The Land and People of

KOREA

The Land and People of®
KOREA

by S. E. Solberg

HarperCollins*Publishers*

Country maps by Robert Romagnoli.

Every effort has been made to locate the copyright holders of all copyrighted materials and secure the necessary permission to reproduce them. In the event of any questions arising as to their use, the publisher will be glad to make necessary changes in future printings and editions.

The maps on pages 36 and 46 are reprinted by permission of the publishers from *A New History of Korea*, by Ki-Baik Lee, English translation by Edward W. Wagner with Edward J. Schultz, Cambridge, Mass.: Harvard University Press for the Harvard-Yenching Institute, copyright © 1984 by Edward W. Wagner.

The passage on pages 25-26 is from Younghill Kang's *The Grass Roof*. We thank Lucy Kang Sammis for permission to use her father's work.

The maps on pages 10 and 127 are reprinted by permission of the Library of Congress and copyrighted in the name of the Secretary of the Army. The map on page 127 originally appeared in *North Korea: A Country Study*, edited by Frederica M. Bunge (Washington: GPO for the American University, 1981). The map on page 10 originally appeared in *South Korea: A Country Study*, edited by Frederica M. Bunge (Washington: GPO for the American University, 1982).

1 2 3 4 5 6 7 8 9 10
First Edition

Library of Congress Cataloging-in-Publication Data
Solberg, S.E. (Sammy Edward), date
    The land and people of Korea / by S.E. Solberg.
        p.   cm.—(Portraits of the nations series)
    Includes bibliographical references.
        Summary: An introduction to the history, government, traditions, and way of life of the
people of Korea.
        ISBN 0-397-32330-1.—ISBN 0-397-32331-X (lib. bdg.)
        1. Korea—History—Juvenile literature. [1. Korea.] I. Title. II. Series.
DS907.4.S65   1991   90-5952
951.9—dc20   CIP
                                                                                                 AC

As fish forget the water in which they live, as men forget the air that they breathe, even so Koreans are not usually aware of Paektu Mountain. The air that has cooled the people's brows from the beginning of time is the wind from Paektu Mountain. The water that has quenched their thirst is from the spring of Paektu Mountain. Everything that is cultivated, planted, harvested, or milled is the product of the soil of Paektu Mountain. It is vain for us Koreans to try to step out from under its influence. . . . The ties that bind us to Paektu Mountain are truly hard to break or dispel. Paektu Mountain exists there on the spot whether we visit it or not; even should we try to escape from it, Paektu Mountain pursues us night and day. Paektu Mountain and us, we are of a single origin, not two.

    —Yuktan, Ch'oe Nam-sŏn. Modified from his book *Paektusan kwanch'amgi* written in 1926–27.

To the people of Korea who have suffered more than they should;
may this generation see within its lifetime a nation spiritually and politically whole
where the wounds of war and division have been healed
by the spirit of reconciliation.

Contents

THE WORLD

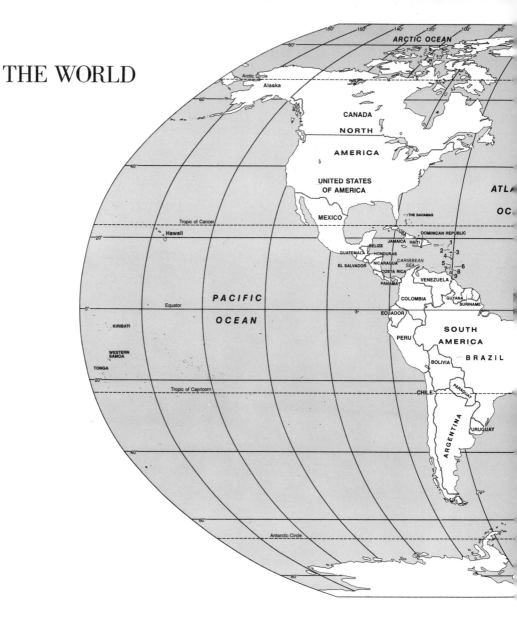

This world map is based on a projection developed by Arthur H. Robinson. The shape of each country and its size, relative to other countries, are more accurately expressed here than in previous maps. The map also gives equal importance to all of the continents, instead of placing North America at the center of the world. *Used by permission of the Foreign Policy Association.*

Legend

―――― International boundaries

-------- Disputed or undefined boundaries

Projection: Robinson

0	1000	2000	3000 Miles
0	1000	2000	3000 Kilometers

Caribbean Nations

1. Anguilla
2. St. Christopher and Nevis
3. Antigua and Barbuda
4. Dominica
5. St. Lucia
6. Barbados
7. St. Vincent
8. Grenada
9. Trinidad and Tobago

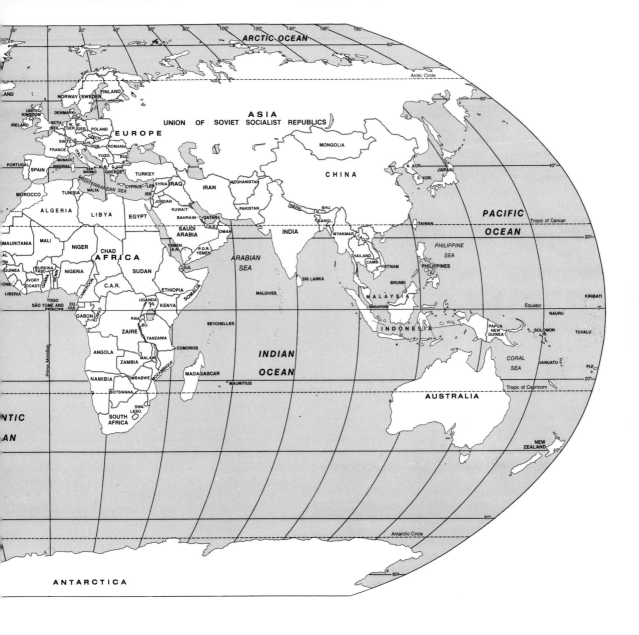

Abbreviations

ALB.	—Albania	C.A.R.	—Central African Republic	LEB.	—Lebanon	RWA.	—Rwanda
AUS.	—Austria	CZECH.	—Czechoslovakia	LESO.	—Lesotho	S. KOR.	—South Korea
BANGL.	—Bangladesh	DJI.	—Djibouti	LIE.	—Liechtenstein	SWA.	—Swaziland
BEL.	—Belgium	E.GER.	—East Germany	LUX.	—Luxemburg	SWITZ.	—Switzerland
BHU.	—Bhutan	EQ. GUI.	—Equatorial Guinea	NETH.	—Netherlands	U.A.E.	—United Arab Emirates
BU.	—Burundi	GUI. BIS.	—Guinea Bissau	N. KOR.	—North Korea	W. GER.	—West Germany
BUL.	—Bulgaria	HUN.	—Hungary	P.D.R.–YEMEN	—People's Democratic	YEMEN A.R.	—Yemen Arab Republic
CAMB.	—Cambodia	ISR.	—Israel		Republic of Yemen	YUGO.	—Yugoslavia

Mini Facts

COUNTRY NAME

FORMAL NAME: Democratic People's Republic of Korea

SHORT FORM: North Korea or DPRK

CAPITAL: P'yŏngyang

GEOGRAPHY

AREA: 47,724 square miles (122,370 square kilometers), about the size of Mississippi

TOPOGRAPHY: About 80 percent mountain ranges and uplands. All Korean mountains over 6,600 feet (2,000 meters) high are in North Korea, including Mount Paektu, 9,055 feet (2,744 meters).

CLIMATE: Winters are long, cold, and dry, summers short, hot, and humid. 60 percent of rainfall in summer.

COUNTRY NAME

FORMAL NAME: Republic of Korea

SHORT FORM: South Korea or ROK

CAPITAL: Seoul

GEOGRAPHY

AREA: 38,406 square miles (98,477 square kilometers), about the size of Indiana.

TOPOGRAPHY: About 70 percent of land area consists of mountains and uplands. Principal ranges are T'aebaek Range and Sobaek Range. Tallest mountain is Mount Halla at 6,396 feet (1,950 meters), a volcanic cone located on Cheju Island.

CLIMATE: Subtropical (Cheju Island) to long, dry winters and hot, rainy summers farther north.

Pronunciation of Korean Names and Words

The Korean language is written in *han'gŭl,* the Korean alphabet, or a mixed script of *han'gŭl* and Chinese characters. It does not use the Roman alphabet, which, with slight variation, is standard for English and many European languages. Transposing the sounds and spellings of Korean into the Roman alphabet is known as romanization or transliteration. Several sounds that occur in Korean and have letters to represent them have only rough equivalents in American English. Some writers have used diacritical marks to indicate these, while others have spelled them in the way they think comes closest to the sound. This obviously can be confusing when the same place name is spelled differently in different books or from one map to the next. You need to be aware of this as you go on reading about Korea. To our eyes "Paek" and "Baek" seem quite different, as do "Kim" and "Gim," but they are variations on the same Korean surnames, just as "Busan" and "Pusan" are for the southern port city.

The romanization system used in this book is the McCune-Reischauer System, which is standard in the United States and the Republic of Korea. This system is used by most libraries for their card catalogues and in many reference books. Except for some place and personal names (Seoul, Roh Tae Woo, which would be Sŏ'ul and No T'ae-u in McCune-Reischauer romanization) that have long-established other romanizations or, in the case of a personal name, reflect the use and preference of the person involved, all Korean words and names follow that system.

The single-letter consonants are pronounced much as in English except softer. Linguists put it this way: An apostrophe after the consonants k, ch, t, or p indicates strong aspiration, but an apostrophe after n, g, or a vowel indicates syllabification in instances where this might be confusing. Thus in "P'yŏng'an" the *P'* indicates an aspirated p—that is, the pronunciation is closer to our p than the softer, unaspirated version, closer to our b—and the *g'* marks the end of the syllable. The vowels should be pronounced fully and distinctly, not slurred, somewhat as follows:

a	as in *fa*ther, p*o*t, c*o*llege
ae	as in m*a*t or *a*dd
e	as in *e*nd or b*e*t
i	as in s*ee* or s*ea*t
o	as in f*o*rd or f*o*rt
ŏ	as in *u*p or s*o*n
u	as in f*oo*d or m*oo*d
ŭ	as in b*oo*k

Names

Korean names indicate more than who a person's parents are. Traditionally a person's name had three parts: a family name; a generational name assigned by a family register to each group of descendants from the founder of the family; and a personal name given by the child's father or grandfather. When a Korean became an adult, he (only men had this chance until recently) could choose another name, called a *ho*, or "style," name. This was the name the mature person wanted to be known by. A woman would be known as her husband's wife or the mother of her eldest son. The convention in romanization is to write the *ho* as one name, the family name as one name, and to hyphenate the given name.

Any well-known figure from the past can equally well be indicated by his (or her) *ho* or by the full name: No'gye is the *ho* of the well-known poet Pak Il-lo (1561–1642), which would be written No'gye, Pak Il-lo. The *ho* is assumed at maturity, sometimes chosen by the individual, sometimes given by friends. It then becomes his name, used alone by close friends, used in conjunction with a title or honorific such as "Master" by others. This name very frequently reflects some ideal trait of character or personality.

Besides the many variations possible in romanization, there is the question of how, and when, the Korean words for mountain, island, river, province, and so on, are to be romanized as part of a place name and when they are to be translated into their English equivalents. Unfortunately, practice varies widely. What we will call throughout this book South Kyŏngsang Province might appear elsewhere as South Kyŏngsang-do or South Kyŏngsangdo or Kyŏngsang-namdo, *do* meaning "province" in Korean, *nam* meaning "south." North Kyŏngsang Province then might come out Kyŏngsangbuk-do, *buk* meaning "north."

To add to the non-Korean speaker's confusion, there is the homophone *do* that means "island" and often remains attached to the romanized names of islands; thus, Cheju Island might appear as Cheju-do or, even Cheju-do Island. The Korean word for mountain is *san,* and it frequently remains in the romanization, so that we have Mount Paektu-san, Paektusan Mountain, and so on. It requires a little care, perhaps even occasional reference to a good map, or cross-checking with another book, to be sure the spelling you have before you is a simple variant and not a different name for a different place. But, confusing as it may appear at first, things soon sort themselves out.

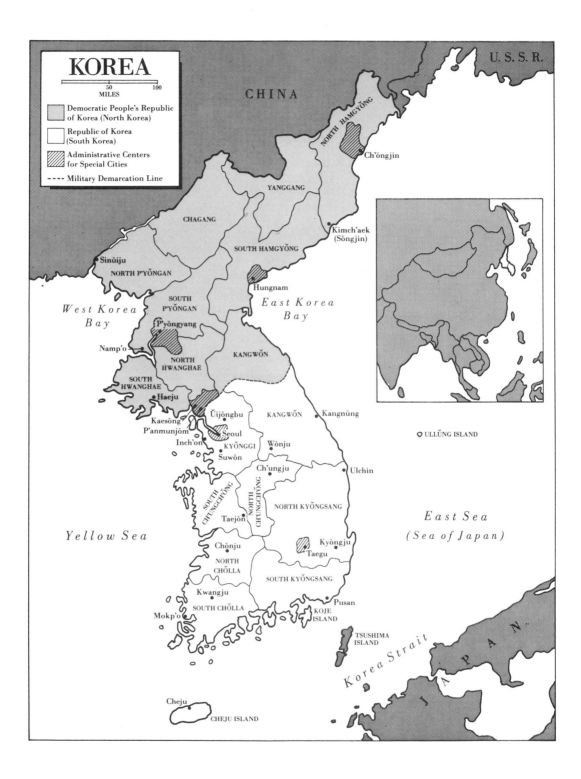

KOREA

50   100
MILES

Democratic People's Republic
of Korea (North Korea)

Republic of Korea
(South Korea)

Administrative Centers
for Special Cities

- - - - Military Demarcation Line

U. S. S. R.

CHINA

NORTH HAMGYŎNG

Ch'ŏngjin

YANGGANG

CHAGANG

Kimch'aek
(Sŏngjin)

SOUTH HAMGYŎNG

Sinŭiju

NORTH P'YŎNGAN

SOUTH
P'YŎNGAN

West Korea
Bay

East Korea
Bay

Hungnam

P'yŏngyang

Namp'o

KANGWŎN

NORTH
HWANGHAE

SOUTH
HWANGHAE

Haeju

Kaesŏng

Ŭijŏngbu

KANGWŎN

Kangnŭng

P'anmunjŏm

Seoul

Inch'on

KYŎNGGI

Wŏnju

Suwŏn

ULLŬNG ISLAND

Ch'ungju

Ulchin

NORTH
CH'UNGCH'ŎNG

SOUTH
CH'UNGCH'ŎNG

NORTH KYŎNGSANG

East Sea
(Sea of Japan)

Yellow Sea

Taejŏn

Chŏnju

Kyŏngju

Taegu

NORTH
CHŎLLA

SOUTH KYŎNGSANG

Kwangju

SOUTH CHŎLLA

Pusan

KOJE
ISLAND

Mokp'o

TSUSHIMA
ISLAND

Korea Strait

J A P A N

Cheju

CHEJU ISLAND

Overview

Night and day the South River flows on, yet goes nowhere
In wind and rain, on the banks, Ch'ŏksong Pavilion stands idle yet
flees with time like an arrow.

Manhae, Han Yong-un, 1879–1944

Place in History

The modern nations of North and South Korea have a long history. The Korean kingdom that preceded them was already old when Columbus first sighted his Caribbean island. By the time the United States had declared themselves free from England, the Korean kingdom, seeking its own kind of freedom from outside interference and internal change, had so isolated itself that people in the Western nations began calling it the "hermit nation." "The West"—that is, Europe and North America—knew little of Korea before the 1880's, only the stories told by a shipwrecked Dutchman and reports of French Catholic priests, missionaries who had stolen, or been smuggled, into the peninsula on their way to martyrdom.

During the 1880's foreign missionary, military, and economic interests forced the diplomatic moves that opened Korea's ports to the world. In 1910 Japan, in a modern bid for empire, annexed the Korean peninsula. Known by the Japanese name of *Chosen*, Korea was to remain a colony of Japan to the end of World War II on August 15, 1945. Then, just as Korea appeared to have regained freedom, the peninsula was divided into two opposing parts, North and South. The country had become a victim of the cold war: the conflict that pitted the United States and its Western allies against the Soviet Union and the Eastern bloc nations.

Many older Americans think of Korea as a place where American troops fought from 1950 to 1953 and have been stationed ever since.

The excitement of expectations—the 1988 Olympics: Children waiting along the route of the torch-bearing runners carrying the Olympic flame from Pusan to Seoul. Hyungwon Kang

Younger generations know South Korea as the source of color televisions, VCRs, and compact automobiles; the site of the 1988 Summer Olympics; and the source of one of the most rapidly growing minority populations in the United States. There were an estimated 290,000 Americans who claimed Korean as their native language in 1985, probably a third or less of the total Korean American population.

Strategic Location

Korea is a peninsula cut off from the continent by seas and rough mountains. This isolation has served both to reinforce a sense of unity and to protect the peninsula, to a certain degree, from events on the Asiatic mainland or across the straits in Japan. However, Korea is also located in a strategic position that Manchuria, China, Japan, and to a lesser extent czarist Russia have seen as crucial to their military security. "A dagger pointing at the heart of Japan," the Japanese saying went. Today, even with the changed character of war and a world shrunk by technology, Korea remains the strategic center of northeast Asia, as important to the United States and the Soviet Union as to China or Japan. Across the centuries Korea has too frequently been in the position of the small country caught between major powers, "a shrimp caught between two fighting whales," the Koreans say.

Mongol armies descended upon Korea in the thirteenth century on the way to attack Japan. Japanese armies marched and pillaged the length of the peninsula to attack China, in both the sixteenth and nineteenth centuries. Then, as the power of czarist Russia grew in Asia in the nineteenth century, Japanese troops were dispatched to Korea, presumably to keep the Russians out, and once there, remained until Japan finally annexed Korea as a colony in 1910. Today the peninsula is divided along an uncertain armistice line after enduring the troops of many nations fighting on Korean soil in a hot battle in the cold war.

Purveyor of Culture

But the peninsula has also served as a route for things of far greater value than armies. Korea is closer to the great culture centers of eastern and central Asia than Japan is. Over the centuries ideas, skills, and religions were accepted by Koreans and modified to fit their needs and tastes as they passed down the Korean land bridge on their way to Japan.

How much of cultural importance was brought to Japan from the Korean peninsula may seem a simple enough question, the answers clearly dependent upon the research of historians and archaeologists. It is not, however; it is a question loaded with residues of the resentment of the ruled and the pride of the ruler.

Giving Meaning to the Past

Consider: October 8, 1988, the 1,400-year-old Fujinoki tomb was opened at Ikaruga near Nara, the ancient capital of Japan. Inside this sixth-century tumulus, or grave mound, was found a stone coffin containing the remains of two people, believed to have been members of the Japanese ruling elite. Along with the remains were a number of artifacts, including a crown, that were clearly Korean in origin and manufacture.

What might this discovery mean? It seems clear enough: Either some members of the ruling elite of Japan had acquired objects from the Korean peninsula, or people from the Korean peninsula had achieved positions of power and prestige in Japan. But the search for meaning and understanding is not that simple; questions of national pride enter in, and the controversy that erupted in the Japanese press, and to a lesser extent the Korean, even spilled over into American newspapers.

One extreme view held by many Japanese has been that Japan is a unique island nation, different from all others, a creator not a borrower of cultures. Only grudgingly could these extreme cultural nationalists be brought to admit that their ancestors might have borrowed something from the mainland—Buddhism, Chinese characters, some technical and artistic skills. For them the Japanese Emperor is divine, a direct descendant of the Sun Goddess, as are the Japanese people. At the other extreme would be the occasional Korean who would claim that everything Japanese came from Korea, and that even the Japanese royal family is Korean in origin. The Fujinoki tomb with its dramatic demonstration of the ancient ties of these proud peoples has stirred up both of these nationalistic voices again.

Most people who are more moderate in their views, of course, see the contents of the tomb as a means to study the relationships between the Japanese islands and the Korean peninsula in those times long before either nation, in the modern sense, existed.

While, at our considerable distance from both the feelings and the place, this may seem almost silly, there remains an important lesson behind the controversy. It shows how history, or more exactly, the way we use the findings of history, can change our understanding of the present—just as, for example, the way we understand slavery can color what we think about racial problems today.

Most of those Koreans and Japanese who disagree over the meaning of what was found in this tomb are old enough to remember vividly the days before the end of World War II, when Korea was a Japanese colony. As colonial masters, the Japanese argued that Koreans were inferior and that Korean culture derived from Japanese culture. The Japanese colonial administration even attempted to stamp out the Korean language by imposing Japanese as the language of the schools, government, and business. History texts were written, or rewritten, to reflect these essentially political views.

Once Koreans set about rewriting their own history after the end of

Japanese rule, it was only natural that the new Korean history should be more nationalistic and deeply interested in correcting what Koreans thought of as Japanese lies. What must always be taken into account in reading and studying about countries such as Korea and Japan is how much their feelings about one another affect what they have to say about one another, from history books to political harangues.

On the Edge of History

Korea has, like many other small nations, remained on the edge of history as it is taught and learned in the schools of world powers such as the United States. It is only when events such as American involve-

Setting paving brick for the Olympic Games housing complex. Like the housing for the Thirteenth Festival of Youth and Students in P'yŏngyang, these apartments were converted to housing units after the games.   Hyungwon Kang

A new housing development in P'yŏngyang. Like its counterparts in the South, built for the 1988 Olympics, it was built to house athletes, delegates, officials, and press attending the Thirteenth Festival of Youth and Students. The automobiles are for the use of the foreign guests. Se Hoon Park/The Korea Times U.S.A.

ment in the Korean War or a growing trade deficit have brought Korea to the center of attention for a time that Westerners take serious notice. But what is learned at such times is more about, say, American troops in Korea and less about the Korean people, their lives, their hopes. The Korean peninsula is often seen as important for, as an example, U.S. strategic or economic interests, but not in terms of its importance for the Korean people and their particular needs and interests.

For the Korean people today, the bitter truth is that they live in a divided country that they desperately want to see united again. The Republic of Korea (South Korea) has achieved world respect as a manufacturing and trading nation. The 1988 Olympic Games in Seoul were symbolic of that acceptance. On the other hand, the Democratic People's Republic of Korea (North Korea) remains an unknown to much of the world. True, the thirteenth World Festival of Youth and Students held in P'yŏngyang, North Korea, in June of 1989 drew 20,000 participants from around the world. But many participants came from North Korea's allies, and recent changes in central Europe and the Soviet Union have changed those relationships and will certainly even affect North Korea's relations with postcolonial and Third World nations. Both South and North have their international ties and supporters, though today it seems that the South is increasing its international ties while those in the North are shrinking. Still, there is nothing to prevent their going their own ways as independent nations of different political beliefs—except for a nagging, deeply felt yearning by the people of both North and South for a nation that is not wounded and torn apart but whole and at peace with itself.

CHAPTER II

The Setting

Distant rocks jut straight up to the skies;
Smooth lakes continue far and wide.
The waves forever wash the foot of the cliff;
The winds ever rock the tree tops.

The Buddhist priest Chŏngbŏp of Koguryŏ, sixth century
[Translation by Frits Vos]

The Korean Peninsula

The Korean peninsula juts southward from the Asian mainland toward the southernmost Japanese island of Kyūshū. It runs roughly 600 miles (1,000 kilometers) north to south between the 34th and 42nd parallels north latitude. From a wide base against the Asian continent the peninsula narrows to a thin waist of only 120 miles (190 kilometers) at the 39th parallel, then widens to 160 miles (260 kilometers).

The Sea of Japan, which Koreans call the East Sea, is to the east; on the west are Korea Bay to the north and the Yellow Sea to the south. Korea Bay is set off from the Yellow Sea by the Shantung Peninsula of China, which is only 120 miles (190 kilometers) to the west of the Korean mainland. South of the peninsula the 130-mile-wide (206-kilometer-wide) Korea Strait (sometimes called by its Japanese name, Tsushima Strait) runs between Korea and the southern Japanese islands of Honshū and Kyūshū.

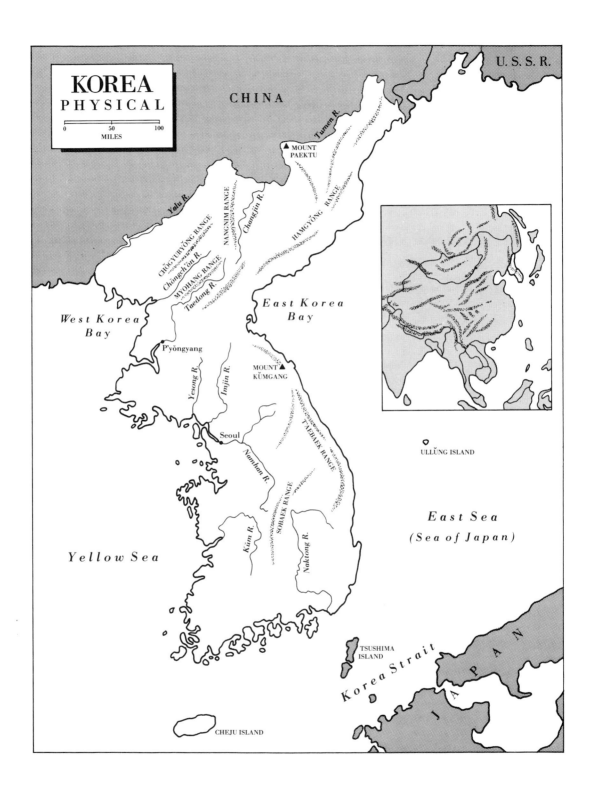

KOREA
PHYSICAL

0   50   100
MILES

CHINA

U.S.S.R.

Tumen R.

▲ MOUNT
   PAEKTU

Yalu R.

CHŎGYURYŎNG RANGE

NANGNIM RANGE

Changjin R.

HAMGYŎNG RANGE

Chŏngch'ŏn R.

MYOHANG RANGE

Taedong R.

West Korea
Bay

East Korea
Bay

P'yŏngyang

Yesong R.

Imjin R.

MOUNT ▲
KŬMGANG

Seoul

Namhan R.

T'AEBAEK RANGE

ULLŬNG ISLAND

East Sea
(Sea of Japan)

Kŭm R.

SOBAEK RANGE

Naktong R.

Yellow Sea

TSUSHIMA
ISLAND

Korea Strait

JAPAN

CHEJU ISLAND

The land borders with the People's Republic of China and the Soviet Union are marked by rivers flowing east and west from Mount Paektu, the White-Headed or Snow-Capped Mountain. The Tumen River (Tuman in Korean) flows to the east, the Yalu River (Amnok in Korean) to the west; backing these rivers are many mountain ranges. The only easy overland routes from the Asian mainland lie along the narrow coastal plains at the mouths of the Yalu and Tumen. The peninsula's 5,325-mile-long (8,600-kilometer-long) coastline has many small bays and inlets but few good ports for oceangoing vessels. Clustered along the coast, mostly to the south and west, are some 3,500 islands.

Over the Mountains, More Mountains

The Korean peninsula is one of the most mountainous areas in the world, mountains constituting nearly 70 percent of its territory. It has been compared to a sea running high—range upon range of mountains like waves chasing each other on a stormy sea. The mountains are always there; living on a rugged peninsula has been the way of life for Koreans across the centuries. *San nŏmŏ san itta*—over the mountains more mountains—goes the saying: overcome one difficulty only to be faced by another. English speakers are apt to picture themselves leaping waist-high hurdles on the way to their goals, while the Koreans view themselves as scaling mountain after mountain along the way and, perhaps, being the better for it, if we can trust the words of the sixteenth-century poet Pongnae, Yang Sa-ŏn:

> *Mountain's high, no matter,*
> *It's under heaven still;*
> *Climb, climb some more.*
> *Man who doesn't climb,*
> *Doesn't even try,*
> *Says: high.*

The mountains that are integral to Korean life are a segment in that great chain (sometimes referred to as the Ring of Fire because of its many active volcanoes) that rims the Pacific, surging northward from the Andes in South America to the Rockies in North America, across the Aleutian Islands from Alaska, then turning southward through Korea and Japan, and on to the island chains of Oceania and the South Pacific. From the beginnings of recorded history Korea's mountains have been seen as a bulwark against foreign invasions, a stronghold against conquest when invasion occurred. The mountains have also helped preserve local customs and regional differences by setting up barriers to easy movement before the days of newspapers or magazines, to say nothing of radio and television. Still, the barriers were not severe enough to prevent the growth of a strong central government and a sense of national unity.

Low hills on the southwest tip of the peninsula gradually give way to larger and higher mountains to the east and north. The southern and western slopes are gradual, made up of plains, low hills, and basins that were formed by the rivers. The eastern slope, in contrast, is steep, with no important plains or rivers as the mountains plunge down into the sea. Only about 25 percent of the peninsula is suitable for farming—mostly the flatlands running along the western and southern coasts. These flatlands have also been the paths for foreign invasions in the past.

Korean mountains form major ranges in two directions, north to south and northeast to southwest. The largest and highest are the Nangnim and T'aebaek Ranges, which constitute the drainage divide, the high point between the eastern and western coasts of the peninsula. All rivers and streams rising to the west of the divide ultimately run

A typical Korean landscape, Kangwŏn Province, Republic of Korea: terraced fields on the hills in the foreground, rice paddies on the valley floor, the highway running in front of the village, and mountains upon mountains in the background. Hyungwon Kang

down into the Yellow Sea, all those on the east into the East Sea. A straight line drawn from roughly P'ohang on the southeast coast of Korea to Mukden in Manchuria follows the divide along the T'aebaek Range to where it connects with the Nangnim Range near the narrow waist of the peninsula. The Nangnim Range runs northeast from this juncture to Mount Paektu on the Manchurian border. The Hamgyŏng Range splits off in a "V" more to the east, following closer to the East Sea shoreline.

High peaks dominate the divide from north to south along the Nangnim and T'aebaek ranges: Mount Nangnim, Mount Kŭmgang, Mount Sŏrak, and Mount T'aebaek. Of these, Mount Sŏrak in South Korea and Mt. Kŭmgang in North Korea, in an area known as the Diamond Mountains, are particularly noted for their spectacular scenic beauty.

Rocky pinnacles pierce the sky around these mountains. Narrow and deep canyons cut through vertical granite walls, their bottoms cluttered with blocks of recently fallen rock and water-rounded boulders over and though which the waters cascade down waterfalls and rush through rapids.

The Diamond Mountains, with views opening out onto the East Sea and many famous monasteries and Buddhist temples, were one of the most frequented tourist centers in northeast Asia before war and the division of the peninsula made access so difficult. Today, with most of the Diamond Mountains in North Korea, there is easy access only to the Mount Sŏrak area at their southern tip, in the South. Yet despite their charm for the tourist or their promise of seclusion for the religious recluse, they and the T'aebaek and Nangnim ranges, of which they are a part, have always been, and remain, a barrier to communication between the eastern and western sides of the peninsula.

The Valley of the Ten Thousand Forms (Manmulsang) in the Diamond Mountains on the east coast of North Korea.   Se Hoon Park/The Korea Times U.S.A.

Running parallel to each other in a generally northeast-to-southwest direction on the western side of the divide are the much smaller Kangnam Range near the Chinese border, the Chŏgyu and Myohyang ranges in North Korea, and the Sobaek Range in South Korea. The Sobaek Range runs down to the southwestern tip of the peninsula and is dominated by Mount Chiri. It has hindered free movement both north and south to the central plains and east and west at the southern tip of the peninsula.

The Kaema Plateau in the north central region, known as the roof of Korea, has an average height of 5,000 feet (1,500 meters) above sea level, about the same as that of much of the Rocky Mountain States. Mount Paektu, located in the northwestern corner of this plateau, is the highest peak in Korea, 9,055 feet (2,744 meters). Mount Paektu's slopes shelter a wealth of rare species of alpine plants and animals.

It is no wonder that mountains have loomed large in Korean life; nor is it strange that the Spirit of the Mountain has been such a central part of Korean tradition and belief. Even the Buddhist temples that dot the mountains devote a special place of honor, a shrine, to the Guardian Spirit of the Mountain.

Despite being a part of the Pacific Ring of Fire, Korea has no currently active volcanoes and is not subject to strong earthquakes. There are dormant volcanoes such as Mount Halla, 6,435 feet (1,950 meters), on Cheju Island, the tallest mountain in South Korea, which was last active in A.D. 1007, and which is remarkable for the pillars, tunnels, and other grotesqueries formed by rapidly cooling lava. But most important is Mount Paektu, famous for Lake Ch'ŏnji, its large crater lake—the lake where, according to legend, heaven and earth meet, the *axis mundi*, the center of the created universe where the

Lake Ch'ŏnji, the Heavenly Lake, atop Mt. Paektu, spiritual center of the Korean people and site of their mythological origins.   Hyungwon Kang

· 17 ·

Korean people and Korean history began with the descent of Hwanung from heaven.

Rivers and Plains

Korea's seven major rivers, with the exception of the Tumen, flow into the Yellow Sea or the Korea Strait. In the past, rivers have played an important role for transportation. One former and two present capital cities grew up as river ports: P'yŏngyang on the Taedong River, Seoul on the Han River, and Puyŏ, the last capital of the ancient kingdom of Paekche, on the Kŭm River. Today the slow riverboats and rafts have been replaced by trucks and trains, and the rivers have become more important as a source of irrigation and hydroelectric power. The dams that made this possible in turn have created lakes that serve for recreation and water sports.

Rivers have been instrumental in the very shaping of the plains that produced the rice and foodstuffs for the Korean people. Just as Korea's mountains are very young in geological terms, so too Korea's topsoils are young, poor, and shallow. It has taken the hard work of the farmers fertilizing and tilling these soils to produce the rich paddies and fields.

A short way upstream from the sea, river valleys narrow. Beyond that point, what agricultural plains there are, are basins formed by a combination of eroding hills and the buildup of alluvial plains where two major rivers meet. Cities that have grown up in these areas, such as Ch'unch'ŏn, Wŏnju, or Ch'ungju, probably are nearly as old as agriculture itself.

Coasts and Islands

The east coast with its narrow plain is quite smooth, with only two major indentations, Yŏnghŭng Bay with the port of Wŏnsan in North Korea

Rivers

Following counterclockwise from the northeast corner of the peninsula, there are seven major river systems. The Tumen River, (Tuman in Korean) runs from Mt. Paektu north and east into the East Sea. It marks the border between Korea and the Manchuria section of China and, for its last 18 miles (16 kilometers), the Soviet Union. Flowing south and west from Mount Paektu is the Yalu River (Amnok in Korean), which marks the border with Manchuria. Farther south the Taedong River rises near Mount Nangnim, then runs southwest through P'yŏngyang to empty into the Yellow Sea at Namp'o. The Han River has its beginnings in the T'aebaek Range and runs generally northwestward across central Korea, joining with its north branch, the Pukhan (or North Han) River, which rises in the Diamond Mountains in North Korea, just east of Seoul, flows on through Seoul, and shares its estuary in the Yellow Sea with the Imjin River, which rises in central North Korea. The Kŭm River rises in the northern part of the Sobaek Range, flowing into the Yellow Sea at Kŭmsan. The Naktong River rises near the Chiri Mountains and empties into the Korea Strait near Pusan on the southeastern tip of the peninsula.

and Yŏng'il Bay with the port of P'ohang in South Korea. Great stretches of the eastern seacoast are rocky, with towering sea cliffs broken only by small sand beaches and spits where short streams run down to the ocean. This is not, on the whole, land to be worked or developed, but rather scenery to be enjoyed: clean beaches, clear waters, fresh air.

The small volcanic island of Ullŭng lies some 80 miles (130 kilometers) off the east central coast. This 28-square-mile (72-square-kilometer) island has the distinction of being perhaps the only inhabited land area in Korea that was bypassed by the Korean War, not having been subjected to aerial attack. Together with its even smaller neighbor, Tokto Island, Ullŭng has been a source of irritation in Korean relations with Japan. Both Korea and Japan have claimed exclusive rights to the rich harvest of seaweed and fishing beds in the surrounding waters, as well as to the islands themselves.

The south and west coasts present very different pictures: an abundance of islands and dramatically indented coastlines. The islands off the southern coasts are the tops of sunken hills left exposed as the seas invaded the land after the last ice age. Farther east Ullŭng and Cheju Islands were formed by volcanic lavas that rose from the seabed.

The west coast has many marshy and swampy areas. The shallow Yellow Sea, true to its name, is muddy. Tides along the Korean west coast range from 20 or 30 feet (6 or 9 meters) at Inch'ŏn near Seoul, to 16 feet (5 meters) at the southwest tip of the peninsula. By way of comparison, tides are only 4.25 feet (1.3 meters) at Pusan on the southeast tip of the peninsula. Such high tides create powerful currents in the narrow channels between the islands, the fastest recorded being 7.5 knots. Tides and their associated currents continually stir up the mud and silt and expose wide tidal flats when the tides are out. Some tidal flats have been reclaimed by diking and drainage for agricultural or industrial use as well as for the salt pans used in traditional salt production.

The Yellow Sea is not very deep (around 300 feet, or less than 100 meters), with a shallow continental shelf. The East Sea has virtually no continental shelf. A branch of the Kuroshio Current, a warm sea current that originates just east of the Philippine Islands, flows north through the Korea Strait and branches near Cheju Island. One weak arm flows into the Yellow Sea, up along the Korean coast, and then loops back along the Chinese coast into the Pacific Ocean. The other arm, which is very strong, passes through the Korea Strait and then flows up along the east coast from Cheju Island to Ullung Island. In the summer months it flows even farther north, to meet with cold currents flowing along the Siberian coast and south down the Korean peninsula.

As a result of the great difference in temperature between the Kuroshio Current and adjoining waters, the seas off the east coast are rich with a wide variety of marine life. The presence of these warm waters also helps moderate winters along the southeastern coast.

Climate

There is a remarkable variety of weather for so small a land area. While all of Korea has what is known as a mid-latitude monsoonal climate, the topography, or shape of the land, as well as the nearness or distance from the sea allow for great diversity. While parts of the south are subtropical, the far north is much like Siberia: In the summer, moist air drifts in from over the seas; in the winter, dry cold air drifts outward from the Asian mainland.

Korean rains are monsoonal; over half of Korea's rainfall (average 40 inches, or 103 centimeters) comes during the three months of June, July, and August. Sometimes as much as 30 percent of the annual rainfall comes in July alone. For most of the country this can mean 15 to 20 inches (40 to 50 centimeters) of rain in three months, more than the annual rainfall in many parts of the United States. Despite the heavy rains, Korean summers average seven to eight hours of sunshine a day. This means it rains very hard in the remaining hours when it does rain.

Seasons are clearly marked in central Korea. Spring comes with the

Temperatures

Around Seoul, the capital of the Republic of Korea, which lies about halfway down the western side of the peninsula, the climate is moderate. The hottest summer months have an average temperature of 77° Fahrenheit (25° Celsius) and the coldest winter months average 23° F (−5° C). In the central far north there are areas where summer temperatures average under 70° F (21° C) and the winter averages are around 0° F (−18° C). On the southern tip the winter averages are around freezing, and there are some areas where many winters will pass without a severe frost. Cheju Island boasts a subtropical climate.

pink of flowering azaleas on the hillsides and the yellow flashes of forsythia. The raw winds of March turn warm, and the hills and fields begin to green. Summer follows quickly, temperatures rise, and by late June or early July the rains have begun.

By late summer the rice paddies are beginning to ripen and yellow, the heat has settled in, and away from the noise of the cities, the constant shrill chirring of the cicadas in the trees makes it even harder than usual to stay awake on a hot lazy afternoon. Rains are over and harvest is approaching. The only dark spots in the sky are the clouds that mark the approach of typhoons from the Pacific. They come most often in August, and usually they miss Korea. But when they do hit, they bring winds and heavy rains that wreck villages and crops and cause disastrous floods.

Wrapping a tree trunk with straw rope for winter protection. Insect pests lodge in the rope, which is taken off and burned in the spring. North Chŏlla Province.   Hyungwon Kang

Autumn months are the best time of the year. The skies are clear and blue—"high sky" is the Korean phrase. And while these clear blue skies may have disappeared behind the smog hanging heavy over the cities and industrial areas, they still are clear and high over the mountains or countryside. Evenings are cool and the days not so hot. It is a time for picnics and trips to view the autumn colors in the mountains, a time when nature is at its best, particularly if there has been a good harvest.

In most of Korea the real cold comes late, around January. The winter snows pile high in the north. In the south there is little snow; yet even there the cold winds that drive down from the central Asian plains chill the air. Then temperatures rise, and the dry cold winds turn raw and blustery. But suddenly the pink of azalea, and it is spring.

Regions

There is more cultural variation in Korea than might be expected in so small a country and from among a people who express such a fierce pride in their ethnic and cultural homogeneity. The difficulty of just getting around on a peninsula with so many mountains resulted in communities going their own ways with little contact with each other. Regional differences in dialect, foods, and styles of houses have been maintained across the centuries.

Just as in other countries, Koreans have stereotyped ideas about people from different regions. These views are often comic and just as often sharp-edged. Often stereotypes are based on dialect, and any speech that differs too greatly from the dialect of the capital, Seoul, marks the speaker as provincial at best.

Connie Kang, who was bureau chief in Seoul for the *San Francisco Examiner* during the 1988 Olympics, commented when she returned that wherever she went on official business, all she heard was "that southern dialect," that is, the dialect of southeastern Korea. That statement reveals much more than it may appear to. As a newspaper bureau chief and reporter she was dealing with people in positions of authority, both in the Olympic Organizing Committee and the government of the Republic of Korea. The fact that a dialect from the southeast was being spoken in those places reflected the shift of political power from its traditional base in Seoul to the south. Regional loyalties remain as important in modern South Korean politics as they ever were in the past. The southwest still retains its own distinction as the center of the political opposition.

In the past, before the massive movements of people from the countryside to the cities and the wrenching displacement of individuals and families up and down the whole length of the Korean Peninsula during the Korean War of the 1950's, regional differences were even more marked. In the first half of this century it was not unusual for a young Korean to grow up knowing nothing firsthand of the world beyond two or three local villages. For many this village world was like the childhood world described with such feeling in his novel *The Grass Roof* by the Korean American writer Younghill Kang, who came to the United States in 1920:

Our village was situated in a huge valley, partly poor sandy rock, and partly fertile soil, between high mountains, covered with pine and oak trees, and many tall grasses. There were streams running down from each mountain hollow, joining the big river which murmured eternity's chant through the center of the valley. A few miles further on, this river passed through the market place where the people of the village went every five days for barter, and there it rushed into the sea. Except for the market place, the people were rural and isolated, and this mysterious water, constantly tumbling in, was the only far wanderer among them. My native village was the kind which all the great oriental sages have thought Utopia in itself. The people had been happy in the same costumes, dwellings, food and manners for over a thousand years, and were like the ideal state of Lao-Tsu, where "though there be a neighboring state within sight, and the voices of the cocks and dogs thereof be within hearing, yet the people might grow old and die before they ever visit one another."

Prehistory

Service of the heavenly master was the most important role in this period; the person in charge of religious roles was also the leader who controlled all the tribal affairs. . . . Among those who served there was one leader who led all the rest. He came from a family that was considered a direct line from the heavenly ruler and served the great mountain.

Adapted from *Asi chosŏn* (1926) by Ch'oe Nam-sŏn

The First Koreans: Paleolithic Peoples

The people who live on the Korean peninsula today share a single cultural and ethnic background. The first known inhabitants of the peninsula came from the north long before there were written records; later, still in prehistoric times, there were migrations from the central Asian plateau and China.

First on the Korean peninsula some 40,000 to 50,000 years ago were a few from among those pioneer bands that undertook that long trek from horizon to horizon, from the interior of Asia across Manchuria, then on to Siberia and on and on across the Bering Strait, and down into the Americas.

Some of these pioneers found the valleys and coastal plains of what we today call Korea to their liking. They were the first dwellers upon the peninsula, settling in such places as Kulp'o-ri in the north and Sŏkchang-ni in the south some 30,000 years ago.

Whether or not these people were the direct ancestors of modern Koreans is one of those interesting questions that may never be answered. The Korean peninsula was not covered with ice during the ice ages as much of Europe and North America was, and temperatures were mild enough to have allowed people to have lived there continuously during the last ice age.

Paleolithic (Old Stone Age) peoples on the Korean peninsula were foragers and hunters: They lived on what they could find, not on what they produced. Mostly cave dwellers, they occasionally built crude structures as well. Tools and weapons were shaped by flaking and chipping stone.

They hunted and fished together; there was greater safety, and a better chance of success, working in groups rather than alone as they stalked larger game, went farther afield. So they lived for thousands upon thousands of years, a life so spartan as to leave few material traces. Then down the peninsula from the north came a new wave of people.

The First Koreans: Neolithic Peoples

People who had developed more advanced tools arrived on the peninsula around 4000 B.C. Round-bottomed plain pottery is found at places where these peoples lived. This pottery, found also in Manchurian sites, points to their northern origin. By 3000 B.C. a new kind of geometric-design pottery (often called "comb-pattern pottery" because the pattern of lines looks as if they had been made by a comb) had begun to take over. These V-shaped, pointed-bottomed pots are the record of a new wave of immigration mixing and melding with the old; they have been found not only all over the Korean peninsula, but as far north as Siberia, the Amur and Sungari River Basins in Manchuria, and in parts of Mongolia.

Time Lines for Korean History

B.C.	Korea	China	Japan	The West
	Paleolithic Age Neolithic Age			
5000				
	Tang'un and founding of Korea (2333)	Bronze Age	Jonon Period	Early Mesopotamia Dynastic Egypt
2000				
		Shang Dynasty (1576–1059) Zhou (1059–221)		
1000				
	Bronze Age Old Chosŏn	Spring and Autumn Era (770–481) Iron Age		Greek City-States Rome Founded (735)
500				
	Iron Age Puyŏ	Warring States Era (403–221) Qin Dynasty (221–206) Eastern Han Dynasty (206–A.D. 7)	Bronze Age Yayoi Period	Socrates (470–399) Alexander the Great (356–323) First Punic War (264–241) Second Punic War (219–201)
200				
	Confederated Kingdoms/ Sam Han			
100				
	Three Kingdoms: Silla (57 B.C.–A.D. 935) Koguryŏ (37 B.C.–A.D. 668) Paekche (18 B.C.–A.D. 660) Kaya (42–562)	Xin Dynasty (7–23) Western Han Dynasty (237–220)		Jesus born

A.D.	Korea	China	Japan	The West
200				
		Three Kingdoms (220–263) Jin Dynasty (265–420) Northern and Southern Dynasties (263–589) Western Jin Dynasties (263–317)	Iron Age Tumulus Period	
300				
		Eastern Jin Dynasty (317–420)		Christianity becomes state religion of Rome (392) Roman Empire split (395)
400				
				Anglo-Saxons established in Britain (449)
500				
		Sui Dynasty (589–618)	Asuka Period (552–645)	Mohammed (570–632)
600				
	Unified Silla Kingdom (618–935)	Tang Dynasty (618–907)	Nara Period (645–749)	Hegira (622) and beginning of Islamic era
700				
			Heian Period (794–1185)	
800				
				Charlemagne crowned first Holy Roman Emperor (800)
900				
	Koryŏ Kingdom (918–1392)	Five Dynasties (907–960) Song Dynasty (960–1279)		
1000				
				First Crusade (1096–1099)

A.D.	Korea	China	Japan	The West
1100				
1200			Kamakura Period (1185–1392)	
1300		Yüan Dynasty (1279–1368)		Magna Carta (1215) Marco Polo (1254–1324)
1400	Chosŏn Kingdom (1392–1910)	Ming Dynasty (1368–1644)	Muromachi (Ashikaga) Period (1392–1568)	Hundred Years' War (1334–1434)
1500				Columbus's voyages (1492–1504)
1600			Momoyama Period (1568–1615)	Martin Luther church reform (1517)
1700		Qing Dynasty (1644–1911)	Tokugawa Period (1615–1867)	Thirty Years' War (1618–1648)
1800				American Revolution (1776) French Revolution (1789)
1900	Taehan Empire (1897–1910)		Meiji Restoration (1868)	American Civil War (1861–1865)
	Annexation by Japan (1910) Establishment of Republic of Korea and Democratic People's Republic of Korea (1948)	Establishment of Republic of China (1912) Establishment of People's Republic of China (1949)		World War I (1914–1918) World War II (1939–1945)

A painted-design pottery that first appeared around 1800 B.C. marked the arrival of yet another wave of Neolithic (New Stone Age) immigrants. At the same time, the geometric-design pottery began to undergo changes in both design and shape: a permanent visual record of the further merging of Neolithic culture groups.

Neolithic man, woman, and child lived mostly in pit houses—pits dug in the ground with roofs and walls supported by posts set around the perimeter—as well as in cave dwellings. Pit houses were dug out in shapes ranging from circles to rough squares. The clay floors were sometimes burned to bake them hard; there were hearths in the centers of the floors for cooking and heating fires. Smoky and drafty at best, such structures still were a lighter, dryer, and better ventilated alternative to the caves.

In time these Neolithic peoples began cultivating plants and domesticating animals, leaving behind little by little the difficult gathering, hunting, and fishing life in favor of a more stable agricultural way of life. At first they lived along riverbanks or on the seashore; later they moved away from the riverbanks and farther inland, where they loosened the soil with stone hoes and harvested the grains they had planted with stone sickles. Agriculture had begun, and with it the capacity to store food for the bad times. By working together and planning in advance, a village group could settle down in one place rather than having to follow the game and the seasons. While the hunters continued going out after game and fish, life had become more settled; the women, the very young, and the elderly remained at the village to tend to their crops and domestic needs. The hides that had been their only clothing were slowly being replaced by cloth woven on the simple looms of the domestic hearth.

Lineage, Clan and Family

People who are described in later records as being descended from a common ancestor lived and worked together as a group. Such a group, sometimes called a clan, would identify itself with an object in the natural world. Even in later times when written records had begun, the Pak lineage group was identified with the horse, and one of the many Kim lineages with the chicken. Male heads of families met to conduct business of importance to the group as well as to choose their leaders. Fishing, hunting, and agriculture were communal activities, as were some religious ceremonies. The group became an independent economic unit, claiming and defending its own territory. Marriage, however, was exogamous—that is, husbands and wives had to be found outside the lineage group, a practice that has been maintained down to modern times in Korea.

As these groups grew larger and larger across the years, they would subdivide. Confederations identified by the territory they controlled rather than their bloodlines began to appear. These confederations continued the practice of choosing leaders by common consent of the headmen of all the families. From these councils emerged the first known chieftains, priests and kings, priestesses and queens, men and women of exceptional physical and spiritual power.

Spirits animated everything—animals, plants, mountains, rocks, as well as humans—in this Neolithic world. People had to somehow propitiate those spirits in order to make their way through life and protect themselves. Their burial customs—and particularly the special care taken to place the dead body with the head pointing to the east, while protecting it with rocks and providing it with items of everyday use—indicate they believed in the immortality of the human spirit.

There were good spirits, and there were bad spirits. There was clearly need of someone able to both intercede with the good spirits and enlist their aid for ordinary people, and protect them against the evil ones, who brought death, disease, and bad luck. People with these special powers are known as shamans or, in Korean, *mudang*. The beliefs and activities that have developed around these shamans are sometimes called shamanism, but shamanism was not, and is not, a formal religion. The Korean term *musok*, which might be translated "shaman culture" or "shaman complex," is more exact, for while there is a ritual involved in evoking the spirits, there is little of theology or the organized hierarchy usually associated with a church.

In a world governed by these beliefs, when things go wrong in life, it seems that some particular harmony with nature and the natural world of gods and spirits has been disturbed. At that point the skills of the *mudang*, the technician of the sacred, are called for to set things right between the ordinary person and the spirit world. This sense of the sacred in all things, the ever-present spirit world, is the common inheritance of all Koreans. Even today the technicians of the sacred, mostly women in modern Korea, play as important a role in the spiritual life of Korea as the technicians of the computer chip play in its economic life.

By the end of the Neolithic period, as bronze slowly replaced stone, written records began to supplement the record of burial sites and the scant remains of long-deserted villages and dwellings. With the coming of the Bronze Age, and the technological developments that accompanied the introduction of that more easily worked metal, change became more rapid. The Neolithic warriors began to consolidate their headquarters in walled-town states. They were able to direct the combined efforts of larger numbers of workers into such communal activities as the building of city walls and the waging of organized warfare.

Old Chosŏn and the Confederated Kingdoms

The sages of olden times founded nations by use of decorum and music. They nurtured culture with humanity and with justice, never claiming undue strength or the help of fickle gods. But when a man appeared worthy of the mandate of heaven, there was often some sign to set him apart from his fellows, showing that here was a man to ride out the shifting tides, take in hand the treasured regalia, and set about the great work of founding a state.

The monk Iryŏn (1206–1289), *Samguk yusa*, adapted

Old Chosŏn: Tan'gun

Korean people have traditionally believed that their history began in 2333 B.C. At that time, so the story goes, the Heavenly King Hwanin's son Hwanung asked to go down from heaven to live in the human world. His father chose Mount Paektu as a suitable place for Hwanung to descend.

Hwanung brought three thousand loyal subjects from heaven; they appeared under a sandalwood tree on Mount Paektu. He led his ministers in teaching people the useful arts, including agriculture and medi-

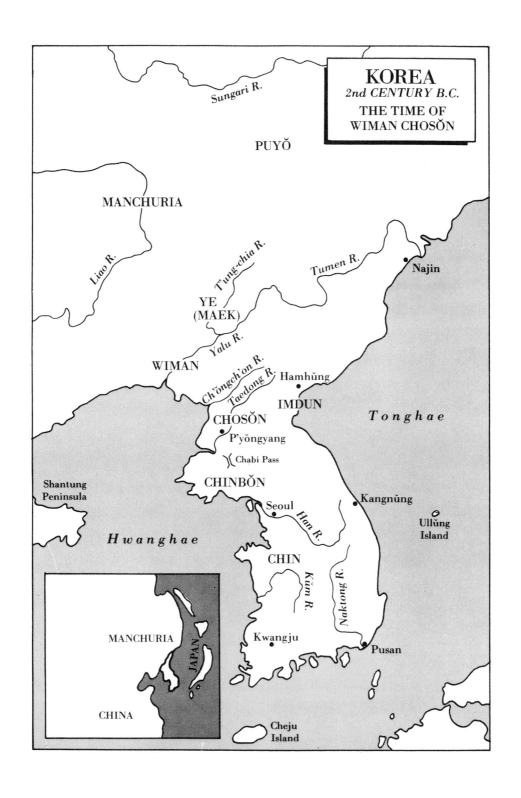

KOREA
2nd CENTURY B.C.
THE TIME OF
WIMAN CHOSŎN

Sungari R.

PUYŎ

MANCHURIA

Liao R.

T'ung-chia R.

Tumen R.

Najin

YE
(MAEK)

Yalu R.

WIMAN

Ch'ŏngch'on R.

Taedong R.

Hamhŭng

IMDUN

Tonghae

CHOSŎN

P'yŏngyang

Chabi Pass

Shantung
Peninsula

CHINBŎN

Kangnŭng

Ullŭng
Island

Hwanghae

Seoul

Han R.

CHIN

Kŭm R.

Naktong R.

MANCHURIA

JAPAN

Kwangju

Pusan

CHINA

Cheju
Island

cine; he also taught good morals and imposed a code of law.

In those days a she-bear and a tigress shared the same cave. They prayed to Hwanung to be transformed into human beings. He took pity on them and gave them each a bunch of mugwort and twenty pieces of garlic, saying that if they ate the holy food and avoided the sun, after a certain time they would turn into humans. The she-bear and tigress took the food, ate it, and went into the cave. The she-bear was faithful to Hwanung's commands; in twenty-one days she turned into a bear-woman. The tigress was unable to comply and so remained a tigress.

Despite her human form the bear-woman could not find a husband; she prayed to Hwanung again, who, upon hearing her prayer, married her. She bore a son who was called Tan'gun Wanggŏm—that is, King of the Sandalwood Tree. Tan'gun came to the area of present-day P'yŏngyang, set up his capital there, and named his kingdom Chosŏn.

So begins the written record. It also indicates that Tan'gun, this priest and king in one, brought together nine of the surrounding groups in forming his new state. Legend sets the date as 2333 B.C. Every year on the third of October, the Korean people celebrate the founding of the Korean nation by Tan'gun.

The archaeological record indicates that the Bronze Age in Korea began around the eighth or ninth century B.C., somewhat later than the legendary birthdate of Tan'gun. The new Bronze Age culture was independent of the slow-changing Neolithic cultures; not only was a new technology being introduced that would in time replace the Stone Age technologies, but a new people were again working their way into that area where Korean culture was nurtured, that is, from the Sungari and Liao river basins in southern Manchuria down into the Korean peninsula.

Bronze Age

Bronze Age culture in Korea is often called megalithic (large stone) because of the widespread dolmen (tombs constructed of two or more stones with another stone resting on top) and menhir (single-stone tombs) that began to appear around the third century B.C.; dolmen burial was common all over the peninsula.

These were tombs of leaders or chieftains who were able to command extraordinary authority over their followers. Erecting a dolmen tomb was no small endeavor; some of the capstones weighed up to sixty or seventy tons and had to be carried several miles to the location of the grave. It took the combined efforts of many workers coordinated by

Dolmen on Kanghwa Island in the Yellow Sea near the mouth of the Han River.
Hyungwon Kang

Bronze Age

The bronze-working skills that came with these peoples were not those of ancient China, where bronze had been used since before 1000 B.C., but rather were skills that had been developed among the tribes of central and northern Asia.

It took considerable time for bronze to replace the stone tools; bronze at first was reserved mainly for ceremonial objects and weapons. Characteristic are mandolin-shaped bronze daggers and multiknobbed bronze mirrors, which are found all across this culture area; while bronze axes, knives for working wood, and spear tips and arrowheads are found, metal agricultural tools do not appear. The geometric-design pottery of the earlier Neolithic peoples continues well into the Bronze Age, but slowly gives way to the plain pottery associated with bronze implements and the new immigrants.

Bronze Age dwellings are often found situated behind earthwork fortifications on the slopes above the river plains and valleys of typical Neolithic settlements. These Bronze Age peoples were more able to support themselves by agriculture, and were less dependent upon immediate access to fishing and hunting; metal weapons gave them an aggressor's edge over existing stone-culture peoples. Geometric-design pottery disappears by the middle of the Bronze Age: The Neolithic peoples had been absorbed into the dominant bronze culture.

Pit dwellings remained the most common housing for Bronze Age peoples, the circular types giving way to rectangular ones with clearly defined areas for men and women. Fragments of cooking and household utensils are found around the inner, or women's, areas of these pit houses, while tools and weapons are in the outer, or men's, rooms.

their leaders to achieve this; it required enormous respect for the dead to even consider the effort.

While the area controlled by any one of these chieftains was probably not very large, it was larger than the simple groupings of the Neolithic period. The presence of earthworks fortifications on hillsides and plateaus has led some modern scholars to call the chiefdoms of this period walled-town states.

By the fourth century B.C. the kingdom of Old Chosŏn, in the region of present-day P'yŏngyang, had expanded its control over the surrounding area between the Taedong River in central North Korea and the Liao River in southern Manchuria. Of the several confederated states that were beginning to grow and become organized at about the same time, Old Chosŏn had the most advanced technology and administration.

Old Chosŏn was located in a region of powerful cultural change and ferment. Refugees fleeing the disorders of the Warring States period in China brought with them the knowledge and skills needed to make iron weapons and tools. (See *The Land and People of China.*) To the north the Xiongnu, the aggressive nomadic peoples of the steppes known as Huns in Europe, were a constant military threat as they pushed down into new territories. (See *The Land and People of Mongolia.*) They brought with them a Scythian-Siberian bronze culture new to the area. These new cultures came together in the Taedong River Basin, where a new metal culture evolved that spread in all directions, even crossing the water to Japan, where it gave rise to the Yayoi culture.

Iron Age

The introduction of iron had led to striking developments in agriculture. Iron sickles made harvesting more efficient, iron plowshares made the preparation of the soil easier. More food was being produced than could have been dreamed of with Bronze Age techniques. But surpluses did not necessarily go to the producers; they were more likely to end up in the granaries of the ruling classes. This was an elite class that rode on horseback or in horse-drawn vehicles, carried metal-tipped weapons, and inspired awe as it imposed its authority through force.

Despite the influx of refugees from strife-torn China and the batterings of the Xiongnu from the north, Old Choson retained its own identity. The bronze and iron cultures may have been introduced from elsewhere, but the techniques of casting both iron and bronze soon became a part of the local culture. It was in this unique blending and adaptation that the cultural strength of Old Choson developed.

Among the refugees to Old Choson from the turmoil in and around China was a man named Wiman, who was of the same ethnic stock as the peoples of Old Choson. Around 200 B.C. he fled with about a thousand followers from the neighboring state of Yen to Old Choson, where he was entrusted by King Chun with the defense of the northwestern borders against the armies of his former homeland. In the process Wiman built up his strength among the refugee populations and between 194 and 180 B.C., he deposed King Chun.

The people and rulers of Wiman Choson, beneficiaries of the new Iron Age technologies coming from northern China, were quickly able to develop the economic, cultural, and military forces of their kingdom in a way superior to those of the surrounding small states, which were quickly brought under their rule. There was a growing government structure with both civilian and military officials; agricultural production was expanded to meet both the needs of a growing population and the demands of a growing army. As the armies of Wiman Choson overthrew the smaller surrounding states, the civilian branches of government grew in order to maintain control of the newly acquired territories and order among their peoples.

Song of the Boatman

While kings and generals left their names and some small record for the future, the little people of Wiman Chosŏn were hardly noted. They were there: the common soldier, the farmer, the trader fighting his war across mountains, through swamps, and over the plains—and the boatman who ferried them all across the many rivers that ran from the high mountains down to the sea. There is a story about one such boatman and his wife found in the Chinese records. Like many such stories it purports to be the explanation of a song.

Early one morning as his boat neared the middle of the river, this boatman chanced to look back to the shore he had just left, and he saw a white-haired old man plunging into the water while his distraught wife stood on the bank and tried to get him to come back. But to no avail; the crazed old man plunged on until he was caught up in the swift current and swept away. His wife could do nothing but sit on the riverbank in tears and pour out her grief in a song.

When the boatman returned home that night, he told the story to his wife, who was so moved that she immediately composed a song as if the incident had happened to her.

Don't try to cross the river, Love, please don't,
I begged, and yet you plunged on.
Dead, drowned in the rapids,
My Love, listen to me, what's left for me to do?

The expanding territories of Wiman Chosŏn soon blocked the overland trade routes between the southern parts of the Korean peninsula and Han China. The traders and merchants of the kingdom, and the boatmen who served them, were able to profit greatly as middlemen controlling trade between these areas. But such control and its associated profit is never without risk.

Wiman Chosŏn was perceived as a threat by the Han Chinese court; war broke out between the two nations in 109 B.C. A year of fierce fighting with the Chinese was complicated by a power struggle within the court, which culminated in the assassination of King Ugŏ (Wiman's grandson) and prepared the way for defeat. In 108 B.C. the capital at Wanggŏm-sŏng, near present-day P'yŏngyang, fell, and with it Wiman Chosŏn.

But these were no great and glittering kingdoms. It is important to remember that the further back from the present, the slower the pace of change. Ten years or less in today's world probably includes more change than five hundred years did in the world of the Stone, Bronze, and Iron Ages on the Korean peninsula. Wiman's Korea was still a mixed stone and metal culture.

The victorious Chinese divided the northern part of the peninsula into four prefectures, the most important of which was known as Nangnang or, in Chinese, Lolang. But by 37 B.C. China had essentially relinquished control of the rest of the peninsula; Nangnang alone constituted the Chinese presence for the next three hundred years.

The Chinese were colonists, living in their metropolitan center separate and aloof from the local population. They exploited the peninsula for raw materials such as iron while returning little. Trade and day-to-day contacts brought the advanced Chinese culture and technology to hand; the people of the peninsula chose what best met their needs.

Some major needs were met by the introduction of Confucianism during this period; one of two major schools of thought in eastern Asia, it also had the unifying quality of a world religion. That is to say, it gave moral meaning to life as well as establishing ethical norms for day-to-day behavior for everyone from king and subject to brother and sister.

According to Ham Sok Hon, spiritual historian and conscience of modern Korea who looks at the past through the lens of a tortured present in his search for the meaning of Korean history, this was a time of toughening by travail, a time of:

... unrelieved agony for Koreans, a dagger stuck in the chest. You can imagine how painful it was to have the land divided with its heart held in hostile hands. How many Koreans fell by the sword, how many died from oppression and exploitation! And how great was the contempt directed at the living, what sorrow and what pain!

And to what achievement: Out of the ruins of Nangnang came the thundering horsemen of Koguryŏ, founders of the first of the Three Kingdoms.

Three Kingdoms to Unified Silla

In ancient days before Silla existed, there were six districts each belonging to a different clan. These were the Yi, Chŏng, Son, Ch'oe, Pae, and Sŏl clans, each of which claimed divine origins. The chieftains of these clans and their families met on the banks of a river known as Alch'ŏn to discuss problems of common interest. They all agreed that it is not good that we live in scattered villages with no protection. "We are in danger of being attacked by strong enemies. We must therefore seek out a noble and great king to rule and defend us."

The monk Iryŏn (1206–1289), *Samguk yusa*

The Founding of the Kingdoms

All the hundreds of small states disappeared in their time, leaving three kingdoms in command of the peninsula. It was not by chance that Koguryŏ, Silla, and Paekche appeared where they did and developed in the direction they did. The peninsula divides into three natural sections. Mountain ranges in the north run more or less east to west, giving a kind of unity across the high plateaus for that rugged country; in the south, on the whole, the mountains run north and south, with a backbone that sets the southern half apart, east and west.

Liao R.

Puyŏ Fortress
(near modern Nung-an)

KOREA
5th CENTURY
THE HEIGHT OF THE
KOGURYŎ EXPANSION

NORTHERN
WEI
KINGDOM

Tumen R.

Najin

Liaotung
Fortress

T'ung-chia R.

An-si Fortress

Yalu R.

Kungnae Fortress

KOGURYŎ

Taedong R.

Hamhŭng

T o n g h a e

Shantung
Peninsula

P'yŏngyang

Imjin R.

Kangnŭng

Ullŭng
Island

Seoul

Bay of
Namyang

H w a n g h a e

Hansŏng

Han R.

Chung Pass

Ungjin

Puyŏ

Kŭm R.

Naktong R.

SILLA

Kyŏngju

Tae
Kaya

PAEKCHE

Kwangju

KAYA

Pusan

Pon
Kaya

MONGOLIA

MANCHURIA

JAPAN

TIBET

CHINA

Cheju
Island

Now friends, now enemies, now combined, now separated: so the culture of the three kingdoms advanced; the movement of trade goods as well as that of persons increased both in quantity and frequency.

To the north was Koguryŏ, 37 B.C. to A.D. 668. From its first capital on the banks of the Amnok River, Koguryŏ's armies overran Nangnang in A.D. 313, establishing a new capital near present-day P'yŏngyang. In its prime the boundaries of this powerful state extended well north into present-day Manchuria and south to the narrow waist of the peninsula.

The formerly nomadic Yemaek, by then turned farmers, occupied the southern part of the peninsula. As a group they were known as the Three (or Sam) Han, a name traditionally associated with Koreans. (It is a different word, written with a different Chinese character, than the Chinese for the Han Dynasty.) It appears today in the official Korean name of the Republic of Korea, Tae*han* Minguk, that is, the republic of the great "Han." The three Han, which were made up of many small village-states, were the Ma*han* in the southwest, the Pyŏn*han* in the middle, and the Chin*han* to the southeast.

In about 18 B.C. a group of emigrants from Koguryŏ settled in the area of present-day Seoul, where they founded what was to become the kingdom of Paekche, 18 B.C. to A.D. 660, controlling the lands and peoples of the whole southwest quarter of the peninsula, the domain of their former host, the Mahan.

Around 57 B.C. Saro, a village-state near present-day Kyŏngju, began the expansion that was to develop into the kingdom of Silla, 57 B.C. to A.D. 935, and ultimately to unify the peninsula.

Koguryŏ

In the north, Koguryŏ, with its fast-moving cavalry and mobile population, became a powerful force in the territorial struggles of northeast Asia—in constant conflict with the Chinese states to the south and west

Koguryŏ warriors on the hunt. Wall painting from a Koguryŏ tomb.   Korean Cultural Center

and the Manchurian tribes to the north. Koguryŏ was an aggressive, warring state, its forces capable of repulsing invasion attempts by the full strength of Chinese arms and even of harboring dreams of aggression against that powerful western neighbor.

Located in an area that had been largely under Chinese control and constantly in touch with the Chinese culture center to the west, the people of Koguryŏ adapted much that was Chinese to their way of life. For while king, court, and people might well have resented Chinese military advances and the arrogance of the occasional Chinese envoy, they nurtured a healthy respect for the cultural and technological superiority of the civilization they represented. Still, respect does not mean slavish imitation. The people of Koguryŏ were a strongly creative people apt at taking what they learned and building upon it.

Koguryŏ Tombs

The most striking physical remains of the northern kingdom have been found in the excavation of tombs near P'yŏngyang, along the Manchurian border, and elsewhere in northern Korea and Manchuria. The bodies were placed in stone-walled chambers that were then piled over with large mounds of earth. These tumuli, or grave mounds, are not very imposing and could be, and indeed have been, mistaken for small, regularly shaped hills; but to pass through the stone entrance is to enter another universe.

Each tomb is in fact conceived as a universe unto itself. The chambers are painted with representations of the sun, moon, and constellations and the appropriate god. The walls bustle with scenes from the dead man's life: hunting, feasting, battles he fought, the wife he loved, his achievements, and his pleasures.

Over the centuries these tombs, easy prey to grave robbers because their stone construction made them so accessible, have been denuded of the wealth of jewelry, ornaments, and other artifacts they once contained. Still, the paintings do remain.

These paintings are riches enough; they pulse with the life of a vital civilization. The artists, with great skill, worked the details of plants and foliage into intricate designs and stylized animals. These are paintings to equal any other fourth- or fifth-century Asian art.

While China was, and would remain, the major culture center that fed into Koguryŏ, diverse elements of other cultures were absorbed as well. In turn this rich heritage—originating from China, central Asia, Manchuria, even Siberia was shared with other peoples; the craftsman's techniques and the artist's skills were passed on to Japan to be once again reshaped to the mold of the users. And in some cases, such as dance and music, the influence of this rich peninsular culture was to make its imprint upon China in turn.

In one of the Koguryŏ tomb paintings a dancer from central Asia, or perhaps even as far away as India, still dances. Before Buddhism came from India to Koguryŏ via China, the dances of central Asia had been woven into that unique cultural fabric that was Korean.

Buddhism was introduced into Koguryŏ from China in 327, later to the other two kingdoms on the peninsula, and by way of Paekche to Japan. It was to become one of the most important of organized religions in Korea, as well as the inspiration for much truly great art. As popular religion Buddhism appealed to the people through promises of salvation, yet it also provided a highly complex and difficult theology for the scholar. Historically Buddhism was like Christianity, a religion to meet the needs of everyone, rich or poor, educated or not, while at the same time, also like Christianity, absorbing elements of the local religions with which it came into contact. Buddhism came to Korea first in its more scholastic guises; but soon the intellectual delight of the monks and the scholars had also become a popular religion with its promise of release from the cycles of human suffering. (For more on Buddhism, see Chapter VI.)

Paekche

The second kingdom of this period, Paekche, was located in the southwest of the peninsula, where, protected from the warlike tribes to the north by Koguryŏ, it did not need to develop a strong army. Though Koguryŏ cut the kingdom off from direct land contact with northern China, Paekche maintained close and generally friendly ties with southern China and Japan by sea.

The Tomb of King Muryŏng

When in July, 1971, King Muryŏng's intact tomb was discovered on
the northern outskirts of Kongju, nested into a low hillside behind
an already excavated painted-wall tomb, it stirred considerable
interest. Not only was this a tomb unravished by grave robbers, it
was also the tomb of one of the great kings of Korea's past.

In the center of the entryway stood an animal guardian carved of
stone sporting wings and a single iron horn like a unicorn's. In the
burial chamber proper, the queen had been laid out to the left of
the king, their heads pointing south—local tradition overriding
imported customs, for in China their heads would have been pointed
north.

Many gold ornaments, pieces of jewelry, a bronze mirror and
bronze censer, as as well as two gold crowns in the shape of flowers
and flames and of exceedingly fine workmanship, were found in
place. The high level of Paekche's artistic achievement was fully
confirmed by this discovery.

As the Three Kingdoms vied for power and territory on the peninsula, Koguryŏ made frequent forays into Paekche lands, and finally, in
475, overran the capital at present-day Seoul. The future King Muryŏng, then a fourteen-year-old prince, fled south to Kongju with other
members of the Paekche royal family; his father was beheaded on the
banks of the Han River by the invading Koguryŏ forces.

Bitter memories of this sad and humiliating retreat led King Muryŏng
to become the great peacemaker of his time when he began his reign

as twenty-fifth king of Paekche (501–523). Indeed, that is what the name Muryŏng means: "Military Peace." He strengthened the military and stabilized the boundaries with Koguryŏ and Silla while at the same time ushering in an era of peace and prosperity for Paekche, in part guaranteed by maintaining close diplomatic and cultural ties with southern China.

Paekche artists and artisans excelled in architecture and related skills, which they passed on to Japan. Examples survive, ironically enough, in Japan, where the Hōryūji temple at Nara was built by Paekche artisans, and the imposing Kudara Kwanon, a graceful wood sculpture larger than life, was worked from a single block of wood by Paekche artists living in Japan.

Silla

It was Silla that was finally to rise and bring most of what is modern Korea under one government, and many modern Koreans would say that the real Korea begins with Silla. Often people find it necessary to look to the past for ideals on which to base present action; many Koreans have taken Silla to their hearts as epitomizing bravery, courage, loyalty, and high intellectual accomplishment.

By the fifth century Silla was pressing hard at the boundaries with Koguryŏ and Paekche. The next two centuries were contentious, with shifting alliances and much jockeying for position. The Tang Chinese saw an alliance with Silla as a way of reestablishing a colonial outpost on the peninsula. In the end, Silla's ability to maintain strong ties with these Chinese was decisive.

The combined forces of Tang and Silla quickly overthrew the Paekche kingdom and then moved against the more powerful northern kingdom of Koguryŏ. Koguryŏ fell in 668, leaving Silla and Tang in control of the peninsula. China, with dreams of colonial mastery still strong, would have liked to remain, and did, indeed, try. Silla, however, proved well able to hold its own in that contest and by the ninth century was in firm control.

Mountains and sea had at first protected Silla from easy attack; for a time the powerful horsemen of Koguryŏ isolated Silla from Chinese and Manchurian aggressors, Paekche had been a buffer against southern China, and, despite persistent coastal attacks by Japanese pirates, Silla had maintained an external peace while building up enough strength to begin to actively expand its national boundaries.

Even though in the beginning Silla had little direct contact with China overland, Chinese civilization still shaped much of people's lives. Confucianism and Buddhism were soon to flourish there; the learning of China, and the practical forms it took in government and administration, supplied the skeleton that the rulers and scholars of Silla could in time flesh out with the fullness of their own distinctive culture.

In the thirty-six years from 703 to 738, Silla sent forty-five missions to China, which included scholars and Buddhist priests, many of whom stayed on to study. Korean scholars from Silla passed the Chinese civil service examinations to serve the Tang government; others passed the military exams and served in the Chinese armies. Most returned home bringing with them their varied experience and broader knowledge.

Commerce   Commerce flourished, with Japan and particularly with China. There, Korean traders were granted special operating privileges by the Chinese authorities. The most prosperous of these trading settlements was in Tengchou on the Shantung peninsula, where the Silla community supported its own Buddhist temple with a congregation of around 250 served by thirty monks and nuns. This Buddhist temple was established by one of the most remarkable of these early Korean traders, Chang Po-go, who built a trading empire from a base on an island off the Korean coast to became one of the most powerful men in Silla.

Silla Culture   A rich and complex culture had developed on the peninsula, where a devotion to Buddhism as both personal and national religion spurred on the arts, architecture, and scholarship. Confucianism, brought back by scholars from China, had direct practical applications in the organization and day-to-day operations of government; it also provided a philosophic and ethical system that was to become central to Korean life during the Yi Dynasty.

Silla's was an aristocratic society where rank and position were clearly defined by the *kolp'um*, or "bone rank system." Only those who, by birth, were eligible to serve as king or queen belonged to the highest, or "sacred bone," rank; the rest of the population was ranked with equally clear restrictions, with commoners and slaves at the very bottom. People were born to their place in society and there was no hope of change: birth, not merit, counted. The government bureaucracy, which since the seventh century had been patterned on that of China, was also very restrictive: Only persons of a particular bone rank were allowed to serve in certain offices. The same was true of the military hierarchy. This aristocratic system would only slowly be replaced by the more open Confucian one, where advancement was, in theory at least, to be on the basis of merit.

However, Silla's leaders made room in both the civil and military branches of government for peoples from nations that had been conquered in unifying the peninsula. Of the nine *sŏdang*, or military units, headquartered in the capital at Silla's prime, only three were of "Silla" origin; three were manned by soldiers identified as from Koguryŏ, two with soldiers from Paekche, and one with soldiers from a Manchurian group. By incorporating the conquered into the kingdom and treating them as equals, the Silla court was able to consolidate its administration over a more truly unified peninsula; there was less effort wasted in putting down resistance by resentful subjugated peoples.

The Hwarang
A group of aristocratic young men who gathered together to study, play, and learn the arts of war were known as the Hwarang. Though the Hwarang were not a part of the regular army, their military spirit, their sense of loyalty to king and nation, and their bravery on the battlefield contributed greatly to the power of the Silla army.

But it was in their devotion to furthering the unity and well-being of the nation as a whole that the Hwarang played their most important role. They went in groups to the mountains—for physical training, to enjoy the beauties of nature, and to make their peace with the Spirit of the Mountain. They were highly literate, composed ritual songs, and performed ritual dances whose purpose was to pray for the welfare of the nation. They also involved themselves directly in intellectual and political affairs.

A stabilizing force in society, they were a group trained together and pledged to the same ideals and goals. It was among the Hwarang that the Silla court could expect to find its leaders in time of peace and generals in time of war. Modern South Korea pays tribute to this tradition at the Korean Military Academy near Seoul, where the campus itself is known as *Hwarang-dae*, or "the hill of the Hwarang."

Hwarang-do, or the "Way of the Hwarang," with origins in the original spirit worship of the peninsula, soon took on elements of Confucianism, Buddhism, and Daoism (taoism) as well. Out of this mixing across the centuries of the three main religions of early Asia and the shamanism of the peninsula came a way of looking at life that was uniquely Korean. Buddhism was the protector of Silla and the following

Koryŏ Dynasty, while Confucianism took first place in the subsequent Yi Dynasty, but none ever totally eclipsed the other, and even unorganized Daoism had more than an occasional advocate along the way. This is, of course, another reason modern Koreans look back to Silla: While they may admire Koguryŏ for strength and Paekche for refinement, Silla alone seems to have been truly Korean.

But however sophisticated the court, Silla remained a land of villages where the farmer went out to the fields every day and came home every night to a village home. Agriculture was the economic base of the kingdom, as it has been for all Korea well down into the twentieth century.

By 918 the court of Silla was dead, sapped by internal corruption and wasteful living on the part of the ruling aristocracy. By 935 even the name Silla had disappeared. A once-great kingdom had surrendered to the strongest of the many rebel forces eating away at its territory.

One of the generals in that force, Wang Kŏn, had had considerable experience in the civilian and military branches of government; he had gained wide respect with both the people and the military. Urged to lead a rebellion to overthrow his leader, Wang Kŏn refused, but the force of popular demand finally placed him upon the rebel throne. Wang Kŏn established his court in Songdo, known today as Kaesŏng, and named his kingdom Koryŏ. In 935 the king of Silla handed over what was left of his kingdom to Wang Kŏn.

Wang Kŏn accepted the abdication with courtesy, treating his former king with respect. And so the kingdom that had first unified the Korean peninsula came to end. A new dynasty had taken power, that of Wang, and a new kingdom ruled the land, Koryŏ.

Ch'ŏmsŏngdae Observatory, built in A.D. 647, is probably the oldest observatory still remaining in East Asia. Hyungwon Kang

CHAPTER VI

Traditional Culture Develops: The Three Kingdoms, Unified Silla, and Beyond

I fear
At this point where life meets death.
"I am going." Before you could finish
You were gone.

Sprung from the same branch,
Like leaves we must tremble, fall
Before the too early winds of any autumn.
I know not where we go.
I shall wait, and cultivate the Way
For the day we come face to face before the Amit'a Buddha.

The Buddhist priest Wŏlmyŏng on the death of his sister. Silla, around A.D. 750

The history of kings and wars tells only a part of the story of any people. The greatness of a nation stands on what is left after the kings and armies are gone.

There were many changes taking place across the peninsula during the Three Kingdoms and Unified Silla times. Societies became more organized, central governments became more powerful, and economic conditions got better. Confucianism, Daoism, and Buddhism among other foreign cultural influences took root. By the end of the period Buddhism seemed almost to be a Korean religion, supported by the court as the spiritual protector of the nation and by the people as a way out of the bitter pain of the cycle of rebirths. Confucianism and Daoism still remained the interest of a few among the aristocracy and ruling classes, while *musok* (shamanism) and the Mountain Spirits retained their hold on the Korean imagination without ever developing into an organized religion.

The pieces were in place for the flourishings of Korean culture. Not until the meeting with the West in the nineteenth century would there again be such a stimulating flood of new ideas and beliefs.

Buddhism

Buddhism first officially came to Koguryŏ in 372, but Buddhist ideas did not make any lasting imprint upon the mobile horsemen of the northwest. In 384 a Chinese monk arrived in Paekche; the first Buddhist temple was built in 385, and Buddhism was adopted as the state religion soon after. Silla was somewhat slower to accept Buddhism, but by 551 it had become the religion of the ruling aristocrats as well as the kings and queens, and thus the official religion of the country.

Buddhism originated in India and came to Korea first through China. It is commonly understood as a religion that teaches that to live is to suffer. Human suffering is brought on because men and women are trapped in a cycle of desire, the fulfillment of desire, and new woes for as long as desire persists. As long as desire for life persists, life persists, even though the person might seem to have died. The only end to

Sŏkkuram, the stone-grotto Buddha. "A supreme monument among all Buddhist art," says one expert.   Hyungwon Kang

suffering, then, is total extinction of the desire for life itself. To achieve that, one must cast off all those things that make up a "self," be totally free of desire, and cut off all attachments to "things of this world." There can be no end to the life of suffering until the flame of the self is extinguished. Otherwise the self is trapped in an eternal cycle of reincarnations. The ultimate state is known as enlightenment, or "attaining nirvana."

One idea that came from pre-Buddhist India, together with this belief in reincarnation, was that the form taken in each incarnation (man, woman, animal, spirit, and so on) represented a punishment or reward for the actions of a past life. Thus the poignant cry of the Korean woman across the centuries: What did I do in my former life that I should be reborn a woman? For it was the fate of the Korean woman to have been born into a society in which a woman was mostly identified by her service to men, particularly in the five hundred years of the later Yi Dynasty. Even the doctrines of the compassionate Buddha as they were taught across the Korean centuries denied the chance for enlightenment or nirvana to any self in female form. Only those reincarnated as males could achieve release.

There are many sects in Buddhism, as in Christianity, and many variations in teachings and practices. There were three major ways of approaching Buddhism, in Silla as well as in the following kingdoms.

The Buddha's birthday is one of the most widely celebrated occasions for South Korean Buddhists. The paths and streets leading to Buddhist temples are lighted by a multitude of brightly colored multishaped paper lanterns as believers, young and old, gather together. Hyungwon Kang

The first, the path most often chosen by the court and the center of the country, said that the way to achieve enlightenment was through a study of the Buddhist scriptures. A second view, the one most popular among the country aristocrats, was that enlightenment came about through meditation, that the study of the scriptures was relatively unimportant. This group is known in Korean as Sŏn (or in English more commonly by the Japanese name, Zen). But by far the most popular of all sects in Silla, and long after, was the Pure Land group.

Pure Land Buddhism is Buddhism for the masses. This was a faith that the uneducated could understand and practice. They did not need to know Sanskrit or Chinese. They had only to invoke the Amit'a Buddha by reciting the formulaic prayer *Namu Amit'a Pul* (I call on the Amit'a [Amitabha] Buddha). This simple devotion was the core of Pure Land teachings. By these means the believer could be reborn (or even directly transported) from this "sea of torment," as the world was called, to the Pure Land, the Western Paradise where Amitabha dwelt.

Another path to enlightenment came through "piling up good deeds" (sometimes called accumulating merit). One of the earliest known Korean poems, probably a work song of the laborers enlisted to build a Buddhist temple, expresses just such an idea:

> *We come we come we come*
> *Piling up the good deeds*

There is a common belief in many sects of Buddhism that the final escape can be attained through the assistance of a class of beings called bodhisattvas. A bodhisattva is a being who has already attained enlightenment but, rather than leave this world, has remained to selflessly help others.

Buddhism showed a way to an end of this life's pain and suffering. It also brought the community together at ritual observances in the temples, afforded a means of release of daily tensions through prayer, and in periods of its strength gave impetus to scholarship and the study of foreign languages. One source says that eight or nine of every ten persons in Silla became Buddhists. While that may be an exaggeration, it still speaks to the power of the Buddhist Way.

Buddhism remained a powerful force for the next five hundred years. Only with the establishment of the Confucian-dominated Yi Dynasty was it to fade into the background. And still today, despite the cries of those who have claimed that Korean Buddhism is dead, Buddhism remains a vital religion in South Korea at least. The temples are busy with monks and acolytes, and there is even a temple devoted to the training and maintenance of nuns.

Shamanism

Shamanism, or *musok*, is the original and continuing core of Korean religious experience. Throughout the centuries a person faced with the kind of problem that seemed to have no known cause would seek relief through the arts of the *mudang* (shaman). In this largely informal setting rituals are spontaneous. They meet the needs of the moment rather than follow a doctrine or text. Some scholars stress that the seemingly timeless trances actually reflect the concerns and imagery of the changing society in which they take place. However, the overall patterns of exchange between the *mudang* and her client may not have changed that much across the ages. Offerings of one sort or another, supplied by the client, are made to the spirit—a chicken, some grain, or cloth—and the *mudang* establishes communication with the spirit as she falls into a trance, often brought on by chanting and dancing to the accompaniment of a drum. The *mudang* will then attempt to find out what the problem is and how it might be solved. The ritual completed, the *mudang* keeps the offerings as payment.

In Korea *mudang* are women, although blind men also make up another important class of soothsayers. The importance of the *mudang* at any period cannot be underestimated; in the 1860's a Korean queen relied heavily upon her favorite *mudang*. Even today, Koreans are liable to turn to the *mudang* in times of distress. While there is certainly more open regard for the *mudang* in the countryside than in the cities, even modern metropolitan Seoul has a district where *mudang* ply their trade.

And for a Korean woman the profession of *mudang* guarantees a kind of independence and recognition that is hard to come by in other walks of life. The power conferred by her special calling sets her apart—when successful, she can make a good living on her own and live her life pretty much as she wants without being constrained by the rules of regular society.

Confucianism

Korea's most influential system of belief is Confucianism. But in many ways it is the most difficult to comprehend. Since its first appearance in the peninsula, which must have been at least as early as the first century B.C., the Confucian system has had an overwhelming effect. In the course of time Confucianism established codes of behavior for the individual, family, and ruler—linked with rituals of respect for the dead. Confucianism also provided the political philosophy for the system of government, and became the center of academic philosophy and literature. It has been said that to write the history of Confucianism in Korea would be to write the religious, social, cultural, and political history of the nation, and in a sense this is true.

There are few Koreans today who would call themselves Confucian, but the structure of their daily life, their behavior toward each other, is derived from Confucian practice. The universities may consider Aristotle more important than Confucius, but the veneration for learning that has led to the amazing development of modern education in Korea is itself derived from Confucianism.

Where the fundamental belief in shamanism is that the good life lies in the proper relations between spirits and humans, in Confucianism the good life is thought to lie in the proper relations and behavior between individuals. Basic to this system of values, set forth by Confucius in the sixth century B.C. in China, was a set of standards by which actions could be judged.

The center was man himself; woman's role was always defined in relation to the male center. Man can become a moral "personality," or a good man, through learning and self-discipline. The good, or moral, man had two main characteristics. He was humane; that is, he behaved in a proper way to the people around him. He also had a strong personal sense of moral duty. By attaining those two things a man became a good man who could make up part of a good society where his example would serve to help others, including women, achieve the same goals. Proper conduct in society was of the greatest importance.

The rules for proper behavior were specified in a set of five relations: of son/father, of wife/husband, of younger brother/elder brother, of friend/friend, and of subject/ruler. In practice this meant that the son must be obedient to his father, as his father must be to the king; the wife must be obedient to her husband, the younger brother to the elder, and the younger friend to the elder friend. Women are reduced to a low position, but men are expected to have a great deal of faith in each other, to be able to restrain their feelings, to hold high ideals, and to approach each other with benevolence.

Songgan, Chŏng Ch'ŏl, one of the best sixteenth-century poets writing *sijo* (short lyric poetry that flourished during the Yi Dynasty), wrote a set of poems illustrating the Confucian relationships at their best. The father's bloodline takes precedence in the jarring first line:

Born of my father, reared by my mother,
Save these two would I ever have been?
Can I ever repay this favor, great as the heavens?

Elder brother, younger brother, feel your skins;
Think of who brought you into the world, made you look the same.
You've suckled the same breast, do not contend with each other.

While your parents live do your all to serve them;
After they are gone it will be too late; though you regret it
Nothing in life will help you undo this.

The Confucian veneration of the ancestors helped make Confucianism popular among Koreans as well as reinforcing traditional ideas about their relation to their dead. The son's, and particularly the first son's, duty to his parent extends beyond life. He must be obedient while his father is alive, and after his father's death he must show his respect in an extended period of mourning and by constant ritual observances on the anniversaries of his father's death.

But it is not only the father who receives this veneration. The dutiful son also pays his respects to grandfather and great-grandfather, as well as to mother, grandmother, and great-grandmother, though to a lesser degree. The ties with the past, and with the family past in particular, are given a deep emotional significance through this practice. And it becomes doubly important that the family line not be broken. The son, if he is to be a good son and good family head, must produce a son to follow him. One of the unquestioned grounds for divorce in traditional

Korea would be that the wife had not produced a son, for a son is essential to carry on the family; he is the link that ties the future with the past, and on a practical level, it is he who carries out the ritual observances across the years.

All the other relationships in the Confucian system are an extension of the father-son relationship. Loyalty to the king, respect for elders, the relegation of women to a childbearing position are all related to this desire to maintain proper relationships. Unlike other systems, Confucianism is not concerned with man's relation to eternity. There is no teaching about a god or an afterlife. Yet it does establish the means for a strongly ethical personal life rooted in the continuity of the family, as well as a proper political or social life rooted in the relationship of subject to king, where the king himself is thought of as a sort of father.

In the Confucian social order as it was established during the Yi Dynasty (1392–1910), which is often referred to as Yi Chosŏn, the status of women declined. A law of 1485 prohibited marriage of widows, of members of different social classes, or of the same bloodline. But not only was a woman's freedom to marry limited; she was restricted by the Confucian principle that required her to be subservient to her parents before marriage, to her husband after marriage, and after his death to her eldest son.

Divorce was not widely practiced, but a man could divorce his wife for any of seven "evils": disobedience to parents-in-law, failure to bear a son, adultery, jealousy on her part, hereditary disease, talking too much, and larceny. Women had no right to divorce their husbands. Women of the "better" classes were not to be seen in public and were confined to "women's work" in the inner rooms of the home.

By way of contrast, in Koryŏ, sons, daughters, and wives had all been allowed to inherit property, and it had been clearly recognized that man and wife owned property together. With the imposition of Chinese and

Confucian ideas in the Yi Dynasty, after the middle of the seventeenth century, inheritance rights were limited to the first son, who was responsible for performing the ancestor rites.

Confucianism, along with all other traditional systems of thought and belief, faced a major challenge by Western ideas of science, philosophy, and Christianity that began to enter Korea toward the end of the eighteenth century. During the final years of the Yi Dynasty it lost its place as a state creed, though the Sŏnggyun'gwan, the national Confucian shrine and academy, remained a center of learning. Despite modern attempts to invoke Confucian principles in the service of democratic politics, the major modern influences of Confucianism are less obvious. Confucianism is still present in the Korean understanding and perception of the proper relations of family members.

Daoism

Daoism is the second most persistent set of ideas derived from the Chinese that prevails in Korea. Like Confucianism, Daoism found the emotional and intellectual soil of Korea congenial and slowly took root deep in the Korean mind. Daoism was a mystic and naturalistic way of looking at life and eternity that appealed to many Koreans who longed for a means of reaching the unknown through ritual or ecstasy. Daoism, as generally accepted in Korea, was not a systematic philosophy or organized religion. Rather, it denied the meaning of such things, celebrating instead nonaction and harmony with nature. Based originally around the teaching of the Chinese sage Lao-tsu, Daoism has taken on many forms. Most frequently it is linked with occult, alchemical, or mystical practices. Daoist ideas were absorbed into other bodies of thought such as Buddhism, shamanism, and Confucianism.

Doctrinal Daoism, which in China featured a search for the elixir of immortality, had little hold in Korea. Together with the associated yogalike practices of breath control, exercise, and meditation, however, it did have a profound effect upon the practice of traditional medicine down to this day. In Koguryŏ and Koryŏ the king offered special prayers to heaven before the Daoist altar, and this practice was maintained as a royal prerogative on into the Yi period.

Over the centuries in Korea Daoist ideas have been freely used in works by artists and poets, by those seeking to escape this world and those who have given up on it, and by religious thinkers and those who find an appeal in the mystic. For the ultimate appeal of Daoism is in the freedom it allows, the fairyland worlds it can conjure—as opposed to the restrictive rules of a Confucian society—and the ultimate power of the wish for and promise of immortality.

The supernatural always delights, and both the Daoists and Buddhists enjoyed stories in which time was obliterated and space contracted. Flying through the air across time and space was seen, in a prescientific age, as a possibility. Daoism led to the growth of much marvelous and occult pseudoscience.

The Daoist did not owe allegiance to anyone, drifting with the flow of events rather than rowing against them, on his way to the Peach Heaven of immortality. Hwadam, Sŏ Kyŏng-dŏk, in the sixteenth century wrote:

This is Chiri Mountain is it;
I've heard much about the stream of Yangdan;
Petals floating over Chiri's reflection in the water.
My boy, could this be the Peach Heaven?

He also wrote:

Silly as I am I do silly things:
Who would cross over the cloud-banked hills?
Still I hark at each falling leaf, each wind.

While by contrast his younger contemporary, the famous Confucian scholar T'oegye, Yi Hwang, wrote:

I make my home in smoke and mist,
The moon and wind are my friends;
In times of peace by my King's grace,
As I grow old my health stays good:
All that I hope for as I go on
Is to live without grave error.

Yin-Yang and the Five Elements

Yin-yang dualism is another central concept for many Koreans. In this view the *yang* (light) force represents male, heat, activity, hardness, and the *yin* (dark) force stands for female, cold, inactivity, softness. These two forces are involved in an eternal process of harmonious interaction from which all nature arises.

Some of the most obvious interactions of *yin* and *yang* can be seen in the alternation of day *(yang)* and night *(yin)* or in the succession of the four seasons. *Yin* and *yang* are also seen as energy modes, as when a burning piece of wood is explained as the *yang* force in the wood momentarily overwhelming the *yin* force. Equal cosmic forces or principles, *yin* and *yang* exist side by side at all times and in all places. At any one time one force may dominate the other, as the *yang* force dominates the *yin* in the burning wood, but overall they are in balance.

Linked with the yin-yang idea is that of the five elements: wood, metal, fire, water, and earth. These are the primary elements or essences that, through their various combinations, make up the universe. They work in a sequence generating or destroying each other according to natural law. Fire creates earth (ashes from burning wood, for example), earth produces metal, metal produces water, and water produces wood, which in turn makes fire. Reverse the sequence (fire destroys wood and so on) and they destroy each other.

Every object, every aspect of life, was assigned to one of the five elements. There is something rationalistic in theories of the yin-yang and the five elements, but over the centuries they have also generated many pseudosciences, among them that of *p'ungsu,* or geomancy, which was to come to greater prominence in the Koryŏ kingdom.

The central idea of *p'ungsu*, literally wind (or weather) and water, is that human beings, as part of the universe, must conform to the cosmic workings of yin-yang and live in harmony with the five elements. The choice of a location for a house or burial place, for instance, has to be such that the free flow of these universal forces will not be disturbed, and the world, at least within the confines of that valley and mountain range, will be able to maintain a utopian balance and harmony.

Koryŏ:
The Wang Dynasty

Rise and fall all belong to destiny.
The Full Moon Terrace is deep in autumn grass;
In the tune of the cowherd's pipe
Lingers the meaning of a five century rule
Bringing tears to the eyes of a traveler
Passing in the setting sun.

Un'gok, Wŏn Ch'ŏn-sŏk, late Koryŏ

The kingdom of Koryŏ, from which the modern name for the peninsula Korea derives, lasted from 918 to 1392. Wang Kŏn was a careful king, not only prudent but a modest man as well. He was careful to make sure he had most of those who counted on his side before he made any major changes. He made it clear that his dynasty was to be the direct successor of Koguryŏ. Northern expansion was basic policy.

One of Wang Kŏn's first actions was the rebuilding of Koguryŏ's old capital at P'yŏngyang, which he called his Western Capital. He wanted to move his capital to P'yŏngyang because of his firm belief in *p'ungsu* geomantic theory, which showed that the natural setting of P'yŏngyang maintained a supernatural energy that could support "ten thousand generations of prosperity."

Wang Kŏn was also a patron of Buddhism who claimed the help and protection of the Buddha for his kingdom while Buddhism was at the same time protected by the court. Temples flourished, and Buddhist monks became influential in government affairs.

The New Aristocracy

With a new king came a new aristocracy, built upon the families of powerful local leaders around the countryside and often tied to the court through marriage. Wang Kŏn established a tradition of consolidating power by taking wives from the more powerful local families that was to continue down almost to modern times. His twenty-nine queens were all taken for political reasons—that is to say, they were all daughters of powerful local families. For the king that meant close ties and support away from the capital; for the ladies and their families it was a shortcut to higher social status and the attendant power and wealth. These aristocrats were patrons of the Buddhist temples and of the arts.

Buddhism

The state-supported Buddhist temples became important landholders. The monks were not taxed; some lent money and some made wines for sale. Temples, many of which were built in spots of remarkable scenic beauty, were tourist centers much in the same way their modern counterparts are today. Buddhism became an economic power as well as a spiritual influence in Koryŏ. On the political side, monks were influential in the court; kings deferred to them, and members of the royal family became monks themselves.

Koryŏ's Buddhists favored Sŏn Buddhism (in Chinese called Chan, and in Japanese by the name most common in English, Zen). The main difference between Sŏn and the earlier Buddhist sects was the approach to enlightenment. Sŏn Buddhists emphasize neither the intellectual study of scriptures nor the doing of good deeds. They search for enlightenment through a highly disciplined process of meditation. Acolytes under the tutelage of their Sŏn master would spend much of their time at *chwasŏn*, or sitting in meditation, rather than reading sacred texts.

Not everyone took Buddhism that seriously. Koryŏ had its religious skeptics, as does every age. The prolific scholar official Yi Kyu-bo (1168–1241), while writing a poem in praise of the new crop of rice and the farmers who grew it, could not resist a skeptic's joke at Buddhism's expense:

> *One grain, even one grain, how could one despise it?*
> *Life and death of men, riches and fame depend on it.*
> *I revere the farmer as I revere the Buddha;*
> *It is hard, however, for the Buddha to revive a famished man.*
>
> Translation by Frits Vos

State Examinations

In 957 Koryŏ established a state examination system, on the model of China's, required of all applicants for government service, military or civil. Although the specific examination questions varied over time, they were always Confucian.

Government service was the final aim of the scholar. It was the accepted way to position, prestige, and wealth. To be a scholar was to render faithful service to the king and the government. While there were two branches of government service, the civil and the military, the civil was considered more important and was granted more prestige.

The Khitan Invasion

The history of the Koryŏ Kingdom is a story of attack and counter-attack, and the honing of the diplomatic skills needed to cope with a complex international setting. War broke out with the Khitan, a Mongol-speaking state based near present-day Mukden on the Liao River, in 993. Although Koryŏ was not defeated in the field, the king was forced to accept overlordship of the Khitan ruler. Early in the eleventh century war broke out again and fighting went on until 1020, at which point relations between the Khitan and Koryŏ became diplomatic rather than military.

The next hundred fifty years are sometimes called Koryŏ's golden age. The kings' inability to centralize power turned out to be a cultural strength. Widely scattered centers of learning grew up around the headquarters of powerful rural families. By the twelfth century, Chinese learning had spread from the court along the length of the peninsula. Small local schools that had been around since the end of the tenth century had become larger and better.

Early in the twelfth century a powerful new kingdom, the Chin, came to power in Manchuria and Northern China. Koryŏ accepted the role of a subservient nation in order to preserve the peace along the northern frontier.

At the same time, Koryŏ maintained a close relationship with the Song court in southern China. Koryŏ's ports were visited by ships—not only those from Song China and Japan, but even those of Moslem countries to the far west. The aristocrats of Koryŏ found Song and Arabian fineries as much to their taste as the scholars found Song books. In exchange, major Koryŏ exports were gold, silver, and ginseng.

The Mongol Invasion

The thirteenth century saw the rise of the Mongol power that was to terrorize the whole Eurasian landmass. Established by Genghis Khan, this empire had spread over much of the Asian continent and well into Europe within half a century. Koryŏ somehow had to find a way to cope with this growing power on the northern border. (See *The Land and People of Mongolia*).

Relations with the Mongols started out well. While Genghis Khan fought the Khitan, Koryŏ gave the Mongols aid. But Koryŏ king and court were not farsighted enough to follow up on their advantage. They condescended to Mongol envoys as though they were their superiors, and in 1231 the Mongols attacked with a vastly superior military force. Koryŏ was badly defeated in the initial fighting and signed a peace treaty with the Mongols, hoping to gain enough time to prepare for further defense.

Once the treaty was signed, the Koryŏ court moved to the fortified island of Kanghwa, just across from the mouth of the Han River on the west coast of the peninsula. Quite naturally, the Mongols became suspicious. It was not long before they returned to the attack in force.

However, no matter how well equipped their armies, the Mongols did not have a navy; they never took the island fortress. While the Koryŏ court never fell to the Mongols, Mongol armies did as they wished on the peninsula, demolishing and pillaging. By 1238 the people of Koryŏ were desperate, and many, following the pattern of their king, fled to islands off the coasts.

The court remained confined on Kanghwa Island; the people suffered: There seemed no obvious way to come to terms with the Mongols. In the Koryŏ court religious ceremonies and holidays were observed even more eagerly than usual to win the help of the Buddha. The court

Invention of Moveable Metal Type

Korea's interest in education, in great part an outgrowth of Confucianism, was also fed by Buddhism. Many books were published beyond the Buddhist texts including histories of the Three Kingdoms and works of many kinds. One of the most important technological developments in this period was the invention and use of moveable metal type in printing, a century before Gutenberg in Germany, during the time the court was in exile on Kanghwa Island. The first book ever published by moveable metal type was a collection of ritual texts by Ch'oe Yun-ŭi, published in fifty volumes in 1234.

hoped that the Korean people would unite against the Mongols through their spiritual unity in Buddhism.

Mongol domination also led to concentration of authority in the capital. The power of the scattered strongmen was broken by the Mongol invaders, who ravaged the country. At the same time, profound social changes were taking place. The military and Buddhist organizations made limited room for people to advance themselves. Commoners were able to hold important positions, and ability as well as aristocratic credentials became a way to advance.

In 1259 Koryŏ came under the domination of the Mongol court, a relationship that continued into the fourteenth century. The Koryo court lost most effective power during this period: Kings were forced to marry Mongol princesses, and the structure of the government was modified along Mongol lines. Officials of the Mongol court resided in Korea as overseers of the Koryŏ government.

The Korean Tripitaka

The Buddha was the protector of the kingdom. Early in the Koryŏ period, in 1011, a Tripitaka, or collection of Buddhist scriptures, had been carved on woodblocks to be printed as a gesture of thanks to the Buddha for saving the country from Khitan invasion. But the invading Mongols had destroyed the original woodblocks.

To replace the woodblocks of that first Korean Tripitaka, the Kanghwa government in 1236 began to carve a new set of woodblocks, which were finally finished in 1251. By the time the woodblocks were carved, the court had capitulated to the Mongols and had returned to its capital on the mainland.

This Tripitaka included many more scriptures, carved on 81,258 woodblocks engraved on both sides. The set of woodblocks, preserved intact at the Haein Temple in South Kyŏngsan Province, could be used even today for printing the Korean Tripitaka.

The Chogye Temple, a center of Buddhist calm in the middle of a rushing city, headquarters of the the largest Buddhist sect in Korea. Hyungwon Kang

Haein Temple, historical and contemporary center of Buddhism in Korea. It is here that the 81,258 woodblocks of the Korean Buddhist scriptures, the Korean Tripitaka, compiled and carved over sixteen years during the Mongol invasion of Koryŏ, are housed.
Hyungwon Kang

Woodblock printing was the most advanced method of book production available. The text was carved in mirror image on both sides of approximately nine by twenty-seven inch (22.9 cm x 68.6 cm.) birch wood blocks which had been specially seasoned to prevent warping. The blocks were then inked, and fine paper was laid over them and lightly pressed down with a brush made of human hair.

There are two major traditions in Buddhism. Hinayana Buddhism, which is found in South and Southeast Asia, and Mahayana Buddhism, which is found in China, Vietnam, Tibet, and Central and Northeast Asia. The Korean Tripitaka (three baskets or containers) is the largest collection of scriptures in the Chinese Mahayana Buddhist tradition. The three baskets refer to the divisions of the material: the doctrine or teachings of the Buddha; the discipline, or monastic rules; and the discourses, or philosophical discussions.

In 1273 and again in 1282 the Mongols launched unsuccessful attacks on Japan. In preparation they forced Korean troops and supporting forces to cooperate with their armies. The ships that were to carry the troops were built in Korea. This created an additional burden upon a country already suffering the effects of extended war, internal revolts, and the continual raids of Japanese pirates.

Mongol domination was not all bad, however. Through contacts with the Mongol capital at Karakorum the culture of the Eurasian world was made available to Korean scholars. Here at the center of a vast empire were brought together the varied cultures of the Eurasian landmass. Scholars from Korea were brought into contact with the medicine, astronomy, mathematics, and other sciences and arts of the West. And Korean culture made its impact as well. The skill of Koryŏ's artists and artisans was brought to the attention of the world at Karakorum.

As the Mongols' power began to wane, the Chinese shook free, and the Ming Dynasty was established in 1368. This brought immediate changes in Korea. An anti-Mongol group used the occasion to have the king disclaim the overlordship of the Mongols and establish relations with Ming. But pro-Mongol forces soon were in control again. In 1388 the Koryŏ king dispatched an army against Ming China.

The king could not have picked a worse time to launch this attack. For years the country had been drained by the attacks of Japanese pirates—raids that at times looked more like invasions as the raiders gained confidence and even threatened the capital at Kaesŏng. There had been constant small wars with Manchurian groups along the northern frontiers. The king and court had done little to relieve the suffering of the people. While farmers were starving, the king and his retinue

Guardian spirit on a door of the Haein Temple.   Hyungwon Kang

would ride across their lands on hunting trips, trampling down the crops. The court was sunk in self-centered debauchery.

End of the Dynasty

During these years of hardship a strong leader, General Yi Sŏng-gye, was coming up. He had helped in putting down the northern tribes and was very successful against the Japanese raiders. A skilled military leader, he is characterized as a furious warrior, a fine marksman with the bow, who was always in the front of battle mounted on his white horse. He fast became a national hero. He was also a firm supporter of the pro-Ming faction around the court.

When the king ordered the generals to march against Ming, General Yi Sŏng-gye argued against the action. He protested that it was foolish for a small country to attack a large one; that the summer was a poor time to begin an attack, for the long heavy rains made roads impassable and the heat and damp would ruin the bows; and moreover, that it was foolish to pull troops out of Korea when the Japanese were continually raiding.

The king's only reply was that the next man who objected to his decision would be beheaded. The troops were ordered to march north. General Yi was seen to weep, for, he said, this meant the end of Koryŏ.

General Yi Sŏng-gye led his troops to an island near the mouth of the Yalu and went into camp there. He did not move any further against China, and finally, after trying once more to get the king to change his mind, General Yi Sŏng-gye put the question to his troops: Should they move against Ming China or march back on the capital? The troops were wholeheartedly in support of the move against the Korean capital.

The decision was made, but even as General Yi Sŏng-gye sat on his white horse watching his troops cross back to the Koryŏ side of the river, he seemed to have had no thought of overthrowing the dynasty; rather, he hoped to save it from what he considered a fatal mistake.

Writing and Literature

There has, on the whole, been only one language spoken on the Korean peninsula since Koryŏ times, descended from that spoken in the first unifier, Silla. But neither Silla nor any of the other early kingdoms had writing systems. China supplied a writing system, as it did so many other things. This would not in itself have led to difficulties if Korean had been a language similar to Chinese, or if the Chinese writing system had been an alphabetic one.

But neither was the case; in the Chinese system each symbol, or character, represents an idea—a word, or part of a word, rather than a sound. For the speaker of Chinese this presents little difficulty: Match the written forms with words already known from the spoken language. But when applied to the Korean language, it was very inefficient. Yet for the most part, while Koreans continued to speak Korean, when they wanted to record something they wrote it down in Chinese.

Silla scholars attempted to adapt the Chinese system to record Korean. The resulting system, called *idu*, was too awkward for general use. Chinese, called *hanmun* when written and used by Koreans, continued as both the language and writing system for most purposes until the mid-fifteenth century. Most of the literature from the Three Kingdoms, Silla, and Koryŏ was written in *hanmun*.

Chinese, especially in its formal written form, was an international language in East Asia, as well as the one in which the major works of the Confucian philosophy-religion and many Buddhist texts were written. Koreans had to know Chinese if they were to study, to learn, or to leave a record for the future.

Written language also had less solemn purposes. Day-to-day life was filled with laughter, tears, love, treachery. There was the funny story to be retold for someone else's delight, and the joy in making it even better in the telling. There were songs and poems of simple things: looking at, recording, saying something about the world and life around and within the poet. From simple beginnings in the recording of folk songs and folktales, on to the writing of complex histories, novels, and poetry, Korean literature grew over the centuries.

Though writing stories or poems was seldom the first concern of the traditional Korean author (and down to the modern period, with a few notable exceptions writing has been almost entirely a man's world)—he was a scholar first, with his duty to his king—once government positions had been put aside and he had retired from the world of "dusty papers," he often would turn to writing poetry for his own pleasure and that of those around him.

> *A clean break with all the papers, well rid of strife and rows,*
> *I returned, whipping my horse in the autumn wind.*
> *What a relief, even an uncaged bird would not feel so free.*

So wrote Chukso, Kim Kwang-uk, an early Yi Dynasty scholar, upon returning to his village home after a long career in office. There youth and age come together for him:

> *Bamboo stick, I'm glad to see you. I rode you*
> *When I was a child. Now you lean by the window,*
> *And when I walk you let me follow you.*

Publication, say in the way this book is published, was not the way in Koryŏ or down through most of the Yi Dynasty. Even though there was the capability of printing both by woodblock and moveable type, the reading public was limited, and books were not bought and sold for profit in the way they are today.

Publication of a man's works often came after his death, in many cases as an act of respect on the part of a son or a grandson, who would gather them together and have them printed to honor the author's memory.

The earliest known Korean writings date from Silla. Most are in *hanmun*, but there are several poems written in Korean and recorded in the awkward *idu* system. These texts were copied, during Koryŏ, from books that have since disappeared.

There are collections of essays, anecdotes, stories, and poetry written in *hanmun* from Koryŏ as well as several long poems recorded in *idu* from Koryŏ's later years, such as this most famous one, "Going":

> *Going, are you really going,*
> *Leaving me and going on your way?*
> *I'll hold you back but then, if I offend*
> *You'll not come back again.*
> *Unhappy lord, I'll see you off,*
> *And as you leave, so come back again.*
> *Oh, the even tenor of our days.*

Divided Loyalties

With the end of Koryŏ came an end to the even tenor of their days for many. Caught up in the struggles for power and the opposing demands on their loyalties by both sides, Koreans entered the troubled transition years to the Yi Dynasty.

Many men at the end of Koryŏ were faced with the dilemma of

whether their personal loyalty to their king was greater than their loyalty to a nation that was badly in need of reform. There was considerable opposition to Yi Sŏng-gye, much of it centered around the person of Chŏng Mong-ju.

Chŏng Mong-ju was a man of gentle ways and absolute loyalty to his Koryŏ king. He was willing to support reforms up to a point, but not a change of dynasty. Sensing this, Yi Pang-wŏn, one of Yi Sŏng-gye's sons, arranged a banquet at which Chŏng was guest of honor. Offering Chŏng a cup of wine, Yi sang:

Come to this side, stay on that,
How will things go all tangled in the weeds of Mansŭ Mountain?
If we were all snarled up like that we might get
nowhere in a hundred years.

In other words, there is no room for neutrality here; you had better make up your mind as to what side you are on. Chŏng returned the wine glass with his response in one of the most famous Korean poems:

Should I die, die again, die a hundred times over;
Should my bones perish—dust and dirt; if I have a soul or have none,
How can my heart ever prove disloyal to my lord?

Once it was clear where Chŏng's loyalties were, it was only a matter of time before he clashed with the Yi forces, and in 1392 he was waylaid on the Sŏnjuk Bridge, where a stain from the blood of that faithful heart is said to be seen even today.

Yi Chosŏn:
The Yi Dynasty

From the heights of Mount Paektu, holding high a drawn sword, I look
Across the lay of the land—hemmed in between aliens north and south:
When, o when, will the dust of strife settle in the north, in the south?

General Nam I, 1441–1468

The Yi Dynasty established by Yi Sŏng-gye, one hundred years before Columbus first sighted America, continued down to 1910, when Korea became a colony of Japan. One of Yi Sŏng-gye's first public gestures after he took the throne was to ask approval of his reign from the Chinese Ming emperor. The emperor agreed and also approved the name Chosŏn for the new kingdom. Thus, unified Korea had existed under three different names: Silla, Koryŏ, and Chosŏn.

Relationships with Ming China were in general good. However, by accepting the lesser title of king rather than emperor, the Korean king took on a junior relationship with China, known as *sadae*. It was like the elder brother/younger brother relationship in the Confucian scheme of things and in time was to cause trouble for the dynasty.

King Sejong, during whose reign the modern boundaries of Korea were fixed and to whose credit belongs the creation of the Korean han'gŭl *alphabet, "the proudest cultural achievement of the Korean people."* Korean Cultural Center

The love story of Ch'unhyang, a lower-class entertainer, and her upperclass lover is the most beloved in Korea. Dating from the seventeenth or eighteenth century, it has been treated in a novel, the traditional song narrative (p'ansori), *films, a Western-style opera, ballets, and more, both North and South.* Korean Cultural Center

In general, the first two hundred years of Yi Chosŏn were peaceful. The emphasis the new dynasty gave Confucianism led to the official suppression of Buddhism, the closing of temples, and the removal of monks from positions of political importance. At the same time, private practice of Buddhism continued, even in the court. It also created a rich intellectual broth that came to a boil in the time of King Sejong, the fourth king of the dynasty, who reigned from 1419 to 1450.

Cultural Revitalization

Stabilization of the country had given scholars more freedom from the duties of government and more time for study. King Sejong brought the best minds of the country together. During his rule rain gauges were invented and systematic records of rainfall were kept; an astronomical office was established that developed many new devices and kept records of eclipses and other related phenomena; a careful geographical survey of the peninsula was made. But perhaps the most dramatic of all was the creation of an alphabet for the writing of Korean.

King Sejong felt the need for a practical way of writing Korean, and after years of study by a group of scholars, the twenty-eight-letter Korean alphabet was completed in the 1440's; many books were quickly published using this new alphabet.

After King Sejong's reign the political situation deteriorated. Factions grew up around the court, each fighting for personal advantage rather than the national good. Many of the scholars who had been drawn into government service in Sejong's time were either in disfavor or had returned to their homes in the countryside to pursue their studies undisturbed by the troubles in the capital. An increasing number of mature scholars turned away from the government to the pursuit of knowledge.

The Thousand Character Classic

The *Thousand Character Classic* was the standard school text for beginners learning to read Chinese, both in China and in Korea. As the name implies, it was a book of one thousand Chinese characters, like any primer introducing simple narrative and basic ideas. Students memorized the text line by line and learned to write the characters. For a Chinese student that was fine insofar as Chinese was his language, written or spoken. For a Korean student a complication set in immediately, since the grammar and vocabulary of the language he spoke were very different. (There were no girls in these traditional schools; they had been separated from the boys at the required age of seven.) He was, in fact, learning a foreign

S. E. Solberg

language, except that the pronunciations he learned for the characters were Korean and very different from the way a Chinese speaker would pronounce them.

The student would memorize his text by rote as the teacher recited it, then would learn to write the Chinese logographs, and finally would learn to identify them by use of a Korean language synonym. What he was learning was grammatically Chinese of the variety generally called classical Chinese. The addition of Korean phonetic letters to the text of the *Thousand Character Classic* was not a way to teach the Korean writing system, but rather a way to expedite the learning of classical Chinese.

The development of the phonetic Korean alphabet, called *han'gŭl*, made things somewhat easier, though the text remained the same even down to modern times. The two pages shown are from an edition of the *Thousand Character Classic* published in 1946, just after liberation. It is printed on the back of wrapping paper from a preliberation Japanese pharmacy in Kaesŏng, for that was a time when everything was in short supply. The idea seems to have been to use the familiar form of the book to teach English as well as Chinese, the old traditions colliding head-on with the new world.

The larger square boxes on the top are the Chinese characters in a clear, handwritten rather than printed, style. The first rectangular box underneath is in *han'gŭl,* also handwritten. (*Han'gŭl* reads from left to right.) Take the second character from the upper right-hand corner, where the English says "house." The first *han'gŭl* syllable to the left above it is *ka*, which is the sound of the Chinese character for "house" in Korean. The second *han'gŭl* syllable is *ch'ip*, which is the Korean word for "house." The next rectangle is, of course, the English meaning of the character. The last rectangle is the pronunciation of the English word spelled phonetically in *han'gŭl.* For "house," then, using the standard romanization, it comes out *ha-u-su*, pretty close.

To the Westerner's eye, *han'gŭl* looks very much like Chinese ideographical writing. This is in part because each syllable is written as a block. But whereas Chinese syllable blocks are based on visual representations of ideas, each *han'gŭl* syllable block consists of a space for two consonants and one vowel in between them (there is even a "null marker" for cases where there is no initial consonant), and is thus a phonetic system and not in any sense a system of "picture writing."

Han'gŭl, like the Roman alphabet this book is printed in, is phonetic—a way of capturing the sounds of the spoken language for the eye. The Chinese characters are not, at least not in the same way. They concentrate on capturing the idea for the eye. The sound that is attached to that idea can be quite different in, say, Japan and Korea, countries that both use Chinese characters in their writing systems, or even between the different Chinese dialects.

The Republic of Korea has clung to a writing system that mixes Chinese characters with the phonetic *han'gŭl*. Every literate adult is expected to know around two thousand Chinese characters. While this usage does reflect a tie to Korea's cultural heritage, it also places an awkward burden on readers. The Democratic People's Republic stopped using Chinese characters in 1948 as a part of a purging of the "feudalist past" and looking toward a revolutionary future. *Hanmun* is a subject for special study. The debate over what has been lost in the process will never be settled until the ideological division of the country is over. Today it is still seen in political terms.

Korean Confucianism

It was in Yi Chosŏn that Korean Confucianism reached its highest development; it was a philosophy based on the teaching of the Chinese philosopher Chu Hsi (pronounced Chuja in Korean) that is usually known as neo-Confucianism. Much of the factionalism among scholars grew out of different ways of interpreting Confucian doctrines, but no matter what the accepted interpretation might be, the only way to advance in government was through the study of Confucianism and passing the civil service examinations.

Confucianism reached into the furthest corners of Korean society. The moral and ethical concepts it taught shaped how Koreans lived. As with all systems of this sort there were those who worked

Confucian scholars studying under the trees.   Korean Cultural Center

wholeheartedly to achieve both the form and the spirit of the ideals, but there were also many who were concerned with maintaining the forms alone. This led to strict rules as to how people dealt with each other that constrained freedoms of expression and social mobility.

Those who did not observe the forms, regardless of whether they chose to ignore them or did not know them, were considered low people and not worthy of notice. It was easy under this system for the higher-class *yangban* (gentlemen scholars who claimed their status by birth) to keep the lower-class commoners in line. While in theory the examinations were open to all, the commoner seldom had the opportunity or time to study the classics and learn all the many nuances of "proper" behavior.

Korea's two greatest Confucian thinkers both lived in the sixteenth century: T'oegye, Yi Hwang (1501–1570) and Yulgok, Yi I (1536–1584).

T'oegye, in the later years of his life, formulated a comprehensive system of neo-Confucian thought for the first time in Korea. The influence of his thought has been widespread—particularly in Japan, where it developed into one of the mainstreams of Confucian thought. Today there is an international T'oegye Society, with headquarters near T'oegye's home in the Taegu area, which holds frequent meetings. A major street in Seoul bears his name, and the South Korean thousand-*won* note—the commonest currency, comparable to an American dollar bill, carries his picture. His philosophy placed a very high value on spiritual, moral, and ethical considerations found by looking deeply inside oneself.

Yulgok, while not discounting moral and ethical concerns, argued that the intellectual values that derived from looking out at the world were most important. The two major schools of Korean neo-Confucianism, which remain alive and actively debated today, have their roots in the thought of these two great sixteenth-century Confucians.

Growth of Private Schools

This scattering of the scholars led to the growth of many private schools. Here Confucianism was taught and senior scholars continued their speculations as they taught their disciples. These schools, which had no connection with official government schools, where students prepared for the government examinations, produced some of the most brilliant scholars Yi Chosŏn was to see. Many of the young men trained there took the government examinations and rose rapidly through the ranks of able civil servants.

The Song of the Five Relations

The Song of the Five Relations is a book of simple, straightforward verses describing the basic five relations of Confucianism and the way they are to be observed. It was written to make the sometimes dry moralisms easier to learn. The poem is printed in pure *han'gŭl*.

This edition was printed in 1931 in Nonsan from woodblocks that appear to have been carved in the 1870's. It is not surprising that such books exist, for they are, after all, part of Korea's tradition. What is surprising is that this book should have been reprinted nearly a hundred years after the process of modernization had begun and well into the lifetime of many people living today.

The section photographed deals with the son's duties to his father specifically, and to his mother by extension, as she is one of his parents. The text reads down the columns, from right to left.

Japanese Invasion

In 1592 the Japanese shogun, Toyotomi Hideyoshi, ordered his forces into Korea as the first step toward the conquest of China. Thousands of Japanese soldiers debarked from their boats at Pusan on the southern tip of the peninsula, and the armies pushed north toward Seoul. The Koreans were hard put to defend themselves. They were caught unawares and unprepared for war; many of their leaders were incompetent, and they were facing a Japanese army equipped with unfamiliar firearms, which European traders had only recently taught the Japanese how to make.

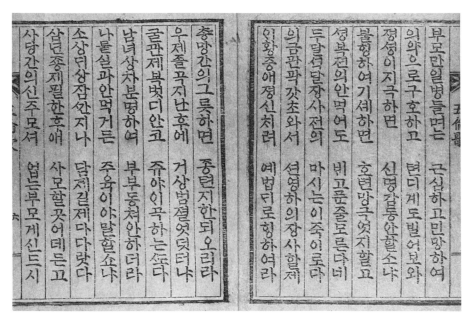

S. E. Solberg

A modern replica of one of Admiral Yi Sun-sin's famous turtle ships that turned the tide against the Japanese invaders.   Korean Cultural Center

Yet while they were losing on land, the Koreans managed to take control of the sea. Admiral Yi Sun-sin, one of the great Korean heroes, utilizing a technical knowledge and skill that were highly advanced for the time, had prepared for just this sort of emergency. His famous "turtle ships," so called because they were armored and shaped like turtles, were invulnerable to attack by the usual methods. They were able to sail right into the Japanese fleet, wreaking destruction wherever they went. As a result, the Japanese land armies were cut off from supplies and reinforcements from Japan.

In the meantime, the king had turned to Ming China for help, and a Chinese army moved in, aiding the Koreans in recapturing key positions. Battle morale was improved, and small guerrilla bands were formed, which scored heavily against the Japanese. By the end of 1593 the Japanese were pocketed in a small area in the south; the king had returned to Seoul, and an informal truce was in effect.

This truce extended for nearly four years. Despite the critical situation, the factional struggles within the Korean court went on, and even the hero of the war, Admiral Yi Sun-sin, was removed from his command. While he awaited his fate, he composed a famous *sijo*:

> *Tonight the moon is bright on the isle of Hansan;*
> *I sit up high in the sentry tower, my greatsword by my side.*
> *Lost deep in care. Of a sudden*
> *A plaintive air from a flute wrenches my heart.*

Early in 1597 the truce ended; the Japanese launched another invasion fleet. This threat brought quick reaction. Admiral Yi was reinstated, though not in time to prevent the landing of the Japanese fleet. Ming China again was called upon for aid.

Once again, things did not go so well for the Japanese. They were repelled by the combined armies of China and Korea. In 1598 Toyotomi Hideyoshi died, and the Japanese armies that were bottled up at the southern tip of the peninsula retreated to their boats and set sail for Japan. But Admiral Yi Sun-sin was waiting, and though he was killed in the battle, his forces took full revenge upon the retreating Japanese fleet.

During the course of the war all major Korean cities had been occupied by Japanese armies. Many had been burned as well as looted, and the material drain on the people was immense. Not only did they have to supply their own army, but the large Chinese force that had come to their aid as well.

Non'gye

Non'gye was a *kisaeng*—that is, a female entertainer—of the southern city of Chinju at the time of the sixteenth-century Japanese invasion. On the occasion of a drinking party, while she was dancing to entertain the Japanese officers, she embraced one of the generals and pulled him with her in a fatal leap off the cliff from which the pavilion overlooked the river. A poem by the modern Korean poet Suju, Pyŏn Yŏng-no (1898–1961) was written in 1924 during the Japanese colonial period both to commemorate that heroic and patriotic act and as a way of protesting the twentieth-century incursion of the Japanese into Korea. It begins:

> *Holy rage*
> *Deeper than religion,*
> *Fired passion*
> *Stronger than love.*

As Korea began to recover from the Japanese invasion, a new threat was growing to the north. A small Manchurian group, the Manchus, had grown strong enough to threaten Ming China. In 1619 the Ming emperor asked the Koreans for help against the Manchus, and a Korean army was sent, only to be defeated.

Manchu Invasions

In 1627 the Manchus invaded Korea. The Korean army was defeated, and the people suffered greatly. The court, however, refused to recognize the inevitable rise of Manchu power and continued to support Ming. In 1636 the Manchus invaded again, causing even more destruction on the peninsula and finally forcing the capitulation of the court. But even after the Manchus had established themselves in the Chinese capital in 1644 as the Qing Dynasty, there remained a hard core of resistance among the Koreans. As the junior partners in the Confucian *sadae* relationship they had pledged their loyalty to the Ming.

Period of Isolation

The terrible destruction from outside attacks led Korea into a period of severely limited contacts with the outside world. Ports were closed; the only contacts were by official delegations to Beijing and Japan, or an occasional diplomatic mission to another country. Korea had had enough of outsiders.

The court, torn by factional strife, lost its power in domestic affairs as well. Intellectual life began to stagnate as it was cut off from new ideas from outside. But not all new ideas could be cut off. The seventeenth century had seen the introduction of gunpowder, more modern weapons, telescopes, clocks, and maps from Ming China, together with books on astronomy, geography, and the sciences, which served as an introduction to what the Chinese of the time knew of Western arts and sciences. By the second half of the eighteenth century ideas from the West, including Roman Catholic teachings, had been carried into the country by members of the annual mission to the Chinese court.

Sirhakp'a

These new ideas were rejected, often scornfully, by the conservative scholars of the official schools. However, these very same ideas helped to stimulate the work of a group called the Sirhakp'a, made up of scholars outside government service. They brought a fresh and more practical approach to learning. The existing social order was criticized. All aspects of life in Korea were held up for investigation and reevaluation. Works on economics, history, geography, and agriculture appeared.

These men on the whole were in both political and intellectual opposition to established authority. The practical results of their work were limited, though one of them, Pak Ch'i-wŏn, wrote a series of famous satirical stories in Chinese. He attacked the existing order by holding it up to ridicule. This description of the *yangban* is typical:

Heaven generates people. The people are divided into four classes and among these four the most honorable one is that of the scholars, also called yangban. There is no greater profit than this. They do not till the soil or engage in trade. Having a smattering of the Chinese classics and histories, one may pass the literary examinations. . . . When his ears are white an umbrella protects him against the wind and when his stomach is fat his servants obey his commands. In his house he keeps lovely dancing girls and in his courtyard he rears whooping cranes. Even a poor scholar living in the country is still able to decide as he wishes. He has the neighbor's oxen first to plough his own field and uses the people of the village for weeding. If somebody behaves rudely to him he fills that fellow's nostrils with ashes, seizes him by the topknot and beats him on his temples without anybody daring to show his resentment.

Translation by Frits Vos

His satire was not deemed funny; the court ordered him to stop writing in his particular style of Chinese on the grounds that it was not approved by orthodox scholars. It is clear, however, that the order was aimed at the stories themselves—the court was not ready to allow this sort of open criticism and used the government's power of censorship to suppress it.

Introduction of Christianity

Christianity—that is, Roman Catholicism—had been of interest to many Koreans from around 1600. Then, diplomatic emissaries to Beijing eagerly began to seek out contact with the "blue-eyed" Westerners, as they labeled the Jesuit priests they met. Catholicism and Western studies and technology, which together came to be called *Sŏhak,* or Western Learning, were enthusiastically welcomed by some Korean scholars.

Books on Western Learning brought in from Beijing were studied by many of the independent scholars, but rejected by the more conventional who found ideas of hellfire and life after death "superstitious." Worst of all, Catholicism, by disallowing ancestor rites, undermined the fundamental Confucian patterns of relations with parents and sovereign. Nevertheless, Catholicism caught on very quickly. By the 1750's there were folk rhymes going around that taught the essentials of Catholicism.

An organized movement to establish a real Catholic congregation by a closely knit group of young intellectuals who called themselves Catholics began in the 1780's. Yi Sŭng-hun (1756–1801), who had accompanied his father on one of the annual missions to Beijing and had been baptized into the Catholic church there, began to baptize others after his return to Korea. Catholicism spread and by 1791 had become important enough to lead to its prohibition and the burning of Western books.

Despite persecutions and a wholesale massacre of Catholics in 1801, interest in the foreign religion continued to grow. From 1836 to 1839, French missionaries worked in Korea, even though no foreigners were supposed to enter the country. In 1839 Catholicism was proscribed again; believers were executed in numbers, and with them the French missionaries.

As Korea's rulers became more and more aware of the pressures of the Western world upon East Asia, they increased their determination to have nothing to do with that world. They had seen China forced to open to the West in 1842, and Japan follow suit in 1864. But like it or not, Catholicism and Western books, and even Western priests, had slipped in despite the determined attempts of the court to suppress them.

As the eighteenth century turned into the nineteenth, strong individuals and families, particularly the extended Andong Kim lineage, were granted extraordinary powers by the king. Since they were not a part of the regular government structure, there were few checks outside their personal honesty to keep them from turning their power to their own advantage. Soon they were exploiting the people for their own personal gain. In addition, people were subject to the greed and corruption of regular government officials.

There were increasing instances of resistance to the government in rural areas, and in 1860 these were organized into an extensive rebellion. It was short-lived, but it required a major effort on the part of the government to put it down. More and more outbreaks of dissatisfaction in rural areas followed. These feelings of frustration and dissatisfaction were brought together with the traditionalist fears of foreign encroachment by Ch'oe Che-u in a new nationalistic religion he founded in 1860, the year Lincoln was elected president of the United States.

Tonghak

Ch'oe Che-u, who himself belonged to the aristocracy, said that he had wandered across the countryside for more than twenty years searching for a way to save humanity. When he was thirty-seven, God spoke to him and showed him a "new way" to save the people.

His new religion was called *Tonghak*, Eastern Learning, to distinguish

Ch'ŏndogyo

According to Ch'ŏndogyo immortality comes through the achievement of a perfect personality in this life, an idea that is more easily understood than an afterlife. The person who has achieved a perfect personality lives forever, not as a spirit or through the achievement of nirvana, but, as in the often cited example of Admiral Yi Sun-sin, in the blood and memory of the Korean people.

To achieve this sort of immortality, a person must live well with others, doing nothing to hurt them. Living this way is the beginning of the perfect life. In Ch'ŏndogyo the world is divided into three levels. The highest is God, or heaven, the eternal or moving principle. The second is the human being, who is the highest of all living things and partakes of the nature of God. At the bottom of the scale are all other living things.

A good person begins to assume more and more of the attributes of God and, in the process, works toward the achievement of a perfect order in this world. The evil person begins to take on the attributes of the beasts and works toward the destruction of the perfect order.

Followers of Ch'ŏndogyo can seem to take a passive approach to life, even though their beliefs were forged out of the bitterness of a revolt against the existing order. Change—that is, life, death, and the beginning of a new life—is the only reality. The final aim of existence is to live in harmony with this unending change. This is achieved not by action, but by inaction (as in Daoist practice)—by doing nothing that will disturb that harmony.

it, both in purpose and kind, from *Sŏhak*, or Western Learning. *Tonghak* was not much concerned with the afterlife; it stressed instead that heaven would be created here on earth when all present evil and corruption were eliminated.

Tonghak became widely popular among the suffering people—so popular that it soon came to cause serious concern on the part of the government, particularly as its followers organized uprisings in the countryside. Persecution followed in 1863, and in the following year Ch'oe Che-u was sentenced to death. But though the movement was banned, *Tonghak*, like Catholicism and Western Learning, remained a major force on the peninsula. Today it continues as a major religion with the name of Ch'ŏndogyo, the Way of Heaven.

The End of Isolation

In 1864 a new king was enthroned: Kojong, whose reign was to span the most eventful days of the declining dynasty. He was still a child, and his father assumed the power of the throne as prince regent, known in Korean as the Taewŏn'gun. The Taewŏn'gun was a complex man, seen by some as a devil, by others as a savior. He assumed his power at a time when the corruption of the court was at its worst, the power of the king was at a low ebb, and effective power was in the hands of the Andong Kims.

In an effort to break the power of the Kims from Andong and reaffirm royal authority, the Taewŏn'gun married King Kojong to a member of the Yŏhŭng Min lineage, which had little political power. He managed in this way to block the powerful Andong Kims' direct access to the royal household. The Taewŏn'gun struggled to reassert the royal power and strengthen the internal administration of the country, but at the same time he was a convinced isolationist and was strongly against contacts with any nation other than China.

This continued isolationism on the part of the court was severely tested by internal pressures: the persistence of the Catholic fathers and believers and a growing interest in Western knowledge. In 1866 pressures from outside began to build up as well.

Early in 1866 a Russian gunboat anchored off a northeastern port and there delivered a request that Korea establish trade relations with czarist Russia. It was ignored. Shortly after this, nine of twelve disguised French Catholic priests who had been proselytizing in the country were found out and promptly executed by order of the Taewŏn'gun. This led to an armed attack on the island of Kanghwa by the French. The French were beaten back.

In the same year an American ship, the *General Sherman*, sailed up the Taedong River to P'yŏngyang, where it ran aground. The Koreans mistook the nonviolent intentions of the crew, as apparently did the crew those of the Koreans, and in the following battle all the Americans were killed. When an American gunboat arrived to inquire about the fate of the ship, the Americans were simply told to go away, which they did. In the spring of 1871 another American expedition landed on Kanghwa Island. This resulted in a fight leading to the deaths of hundreds of people, among them three Americans.

None of these expeditions reduced the confidence of the Koreans in their ability to defend themselves against the power of the Western nations. They had, after all, come out on top in all encounters, and they found no good reason to hold Westerners in high regard. But Korea's isolation was soon to come to an end.

In 1872 the Japanese sent to the Korean court an envoy who managed to open the eyes of some—including Queen Min, who had personally become very influential with the king—to the importance of international diplomacy. Still, the Taewŏn'gun frustrated all attempts at establishing diplomatic relations with Japan. When a Japanese ship was fired upon by the Koreans, Japan made an issue of the incident, and in 1876 sent a military force. Rather than fight, the Japanese chose to negotiate, and in February 1876 a treaty was ratified between Korea and Japan that marked Korea's emergence from isolation.

Development of National Culture

Despite the influence of imported Chinese culture and Confucianism, from early on in the Yi Dynasty there was a strong sense of Koreans being Korean. Down through the dynasty the common people, the peasants and peddlers, laborers and all non-*yangban*, felt an antagonism and resentment of the Chinese-style aristocratic *yangban* culture. In the earlier years of the dynasty these feelings did not surface so often. But after the Japanese invasions when war tore apart the very fabric of society, the vital center of Korean culture was in the folk arts.

Music, poetry, mask plays, and folk painting as they developed among the common people frequently had a broad satirical twist aimed at the upper-class *yangban*. At the same time many *yangban* found these arts more to their liking than the formalisms of upper-class Chinese art forms and gave the popular artists their support. In the late fifteenth century a *yangban* scholar named Nam Hyo-on took obvious delight in his description of the Korean way of dancing:

We bob our heads, roll our eyes, hump our backs and work our bodies, legs, arms, and fingertips. We pull them in tight and spring them out again and again like a taut bowstring. Then we run leaping around like dogs. We tower upright like bears, then swoop down like birds with outstretched wings. From the highest nobles in the state down to the lowest dancing girl—everyone knows these dances, everyone takes pleasure in them.

Magpies and leopard. Leopards or tigers and magpies are a common motif in Korean folk paintings.   Korean Cultural Center

Taehangno, Seoul. College students performing a traditional farmer's dance. There is a growing interest in Korean traditions among students.   Hyungwon Kang

The great good spirits of this irrepressible folk culture are easily seen in many of the brief lyric *sijo* poems from the later years of the dynasty. The poets are not known, but their work stands as a monument to the common people of Yi Dynasty Korea.

> *When I see her I wish I could hate her.*
> *When I don't see her I wish I could forget her.*
> *Or rather, I wish she had never been born,*
> *Or I had never met her.*
> *I only hope I die before her: then she can pine over me.*

This is a variant *sijo* form that uses unusually long lines to create a humorous tension:

What the hen pheasant feels when driven by the falcon to a peak bare of trees and rocks, and
What the captain feels when met by pirates on the wide T'aechŏn Sea in a ship loaded with thousands of bushels of rice when it rains and the oars are gone, the sails lost, the rigging broken, the mast smashed, the rudder torn loose, and it snows, the waves run high and fog is thick all around, and the way home is ten thousand miles and a thousand more, and already the sun is sinking and it is getting dark and all the sea is desolate, and the coming storm is reflected in the western sky, and
What I feel who lost my love a few days ago. What can you compare these to?

But the closed society that nurtured this warmth and good humor was soon to be radically changed by the intrusion of the West.

CHAPTER IX

Taehan Min'guk/Contacts with the West

If foolish, why not utterly foolish?
If mad, why not utterly mad?
Sometimes I seem foolish, sometimes mad,
Sometimes to understand, sometimes not.
Neither here nor there, this nor that,
I don't know what I am.

Sijo by an unknown poet of late eighteenth
or nineteenth century

Korea's treaty with Japan was soon followed by others: the United States in 1882; the United Kingdom and Germany, 1883; Italy and Russia, 1884; France, 1886; and Austria, 1892. But opening doors to the outside world did not solve the problems that plagued Korea. The Korean people were suffering from the corruption and greed of their own government officials. The central government was weak and faction-ridden. The rulers had little experience of international diplomacy, having left all diplomatic relations in the recent past to the hands of China. Korea became a pawn in the international power struggle in East Asia.

After over two hundred years of virtual isolation, a growing number of Koreans began to investigate the outside world. Study and observation missions were sent to China and Japan in 1880 to see what they could learn from the modernization. They came back deeply impressed by what they had seen. As diplomatic relations were established with one foreign nation after the other, more Koreans traveled farther—to the United States, Europe, and Russia—and brought back stories of what they had seen and learned. A small, but steadily growing, progressive group felt that Korea, too, must join the modern world, but there also remained strong conservative elements in the court that resisted any change.

In 1881 reforms were introduced in the military system by bringing in a Japanese military officer to train a new army. This created considerable dissension in the old-line army. The next year the old army launched a revolt. Soldiers marched in the streets, joined by many who had their own grievances against the way things were going at court, and attacked the government buildings. The queen was forced to flee, leaving the Taewŏn'gun in virtual control. After killing the Japanese army officer who was training the troops, the soldiers directed their attack on the Japanese legation, forcing the Japanese minister and his staff to flee.

The Chinese took this opportunity to recoup their position in Korea, and sent troops accompanied by a high-ranking diplomat to help reestablish order. The Taewŏn'gun, who had clearly had a hand in the uprising, was shipped off to China, and when things had settled down, Queen Min, who was generally thought to have been killed in the turmoil, emerged from her sanctuary in the countryside.

One group of young reformers around the court felt sincerely that Japan, which had made such a spectacular success of modernizing since the Meiji Restoration of 1868 (when Japan opened ports to the West), was the force of the future in East Asia; they took the Japanese side in the power struggle. In 1884, with the aid of Japanese soldiers stationed in Seoul, they established a reform cabinet by military coup. The king was abducted from the palace and placed under armed Japanese guard.

An ambitious program of reforms was announced, and it looked for the moment as if the old guard had been broken and a new time was at hand. However, the Chinese envoy in Seoul reacted quickly, sensing there was little public support for the reformers. Chinese troops appeared on the streets, and three days after the reform was inaugurated, the reformers and their Japanese allies were in flight—the king and queen back on the throne.

The China-Japan power struggle around the Korean government came to a head in 1894. An organized revolt broke out, stimulated in

Chŏn Pong-jun (chained to the palanquin), leader of the Tonghak Rebellion of 1894, captured by Yi Dynasty government forces. The inset shows him in the covered palanquin.
Korean Cultural Center

part by terrible conditions in the countryside, in part by a distrust of a perceived growing foreign influence on the government. The Korean government did not have the resources to put down the revolt and asked China for military aid. The Japanese sent troops to Korea as well, and war broke out between Japan and China. In the conflict—the first Sino-Japanese War, in which Japan easily defeated the Chinese—the Japanese took firm control of the peninsula. They forced an unwilling Korean court to accept essentially the same modernization reforms that had been urged before. To conservative Koreans this was a double blow. Not only was modernization being urged by an unwelcome intruder, but people were being forced into sudden and sweeping change.

By this time both King Kojong and Queen Min, whatever their personal inclinations, had had enough of the Chinese-Japanese struggle for control at the expense of Korea. It was clear to them that Japan was simply seeking the position of influence in Seoul which China had traditionally held. In the middle of such trying events they turned to Russia. In a last desperate move aimed at securing their position in Korea, a group of Japanese attacked the royal palace, murdered the queen, and forced the frightened king to appoint a pro-Japanese cabinet.

The new cabinet then proceeded to push through the reforms of 1894, known as the Kabo Reforms. Armed defiance resulted in the countryside, and government troops had to be dispatched to suppress it. These signs of popular aversion to Japanese power did not escape the Russian minister in Seoul.

The Russian minister carefully arranged for the arrival of an embassy guard of one hundred Russian soldiers, and then managed to have the Korean king take refuge in the Russian embassy. The pro-Russian factions took full advantage of the situation. When the king returned to his palace on February 20, 1897, Russia's position on the peninsula was strong.

The Concessions Game

The king and court were caught up in playing one foreign power against the other in order to maintain some balance, but in the process they made promises to the various countries in return for their support. These frequently turned into economic or trading concessions—that is, grants of exclusive rights to a particular country, or even a specific company from a particular country, to certain natural resources, public works projects, or the use of Korean territory for certain specific purposes, such as reserving places to store coal to fuel steamships. In the fifteen years between 1883 and 1898, twenty-one such concessions were granted to seven different countries.

Concession	Year	Country
Right to lay underwater telegraph cable from Nagasaki to Pusan	1883	Japan
Right to string telegraph lines from Inch'ŏn to Ŭiju.	1885	China
Right to string telegraph lines from Pusan to Inch'ŏn	1885	Japan
Right to have a coaling station on Yong Island off Pusan	1885	Japan
Right to fish off the Korean coast	1888	Japan
Permission to have another coaling station on Wŏlmi Island by Inch'ŏn	1891	Japan
Territorial fishing rights off Kyŏngsang Province	1891	Japan

Right to build a railroad from Pusan to Seoul	1894	Japan
Right to mine for gold at Unsan in P'yŏng'an Province	1895	United States
Right to build a railroad from Seoul to Inch'ŏn	1896	United States
All mining rights in two counties in Hamgyŏng Province	1896	Russia
Permission for a coaling station on Wŏlmi Island off Inch'ŏn	1896	Russia
Right to exploit timber in the Yalu River Basin and on Ullŭng Island	1896	Russia
Right to build a railroad from Seoul to Ŭiju	1896	France
Right to mine gold at at Kŭmsong, Kangwŏn Province	1897	Germany
Permission to have a coaling station on Yong Island by Pusan	1898	Russia
Contract for the installation of electricity and water mains in Seoul	1898	United States
Authorization to establish a Russian-Korean bank	1898	Russia
Right to mine gold at Unsan in P'yŏng'an Province	1898	England
Exclusive rights to buy the coal produced at P'yŏngyang	1898	Japan
Right to build the Seoul–Inch'ŏn railroad after buying the concession from the United States	1898	Japan

During this period a number of concessions had been granted to foreign powers. Russia, of course, made use of being the king's protector. Valuable lumbering rights along the northern Korean border, mining rights in the interior, the right to supervise the military training of Korea's army, and, of major importance, the right to handle the finances of the Korean government were variously granted to Russia, Russian companies, or individuals. At the same time, the United States demanded, and received, concessions for a Seoul–Inch'ŏn railroad, for gold mining in the interior, and for a streetcar line in Seoul. Concessions were granted to Japan for a Pusan–Seoul railroad and gold mining; to Britain and Germany for gold mining; and to France for a railroad from Seoul to the northwest border of Korea.

The government's lack of initiative and constant reliance on help from outside nations, with no reckoning of the final cost to Korea, outraged younger intellectuals. In 1896 a group of these men (one of whom, Philip Jaisohn, was American educated and the first Korean to become an American citizen) banded together in a group called the Independence Club, which stood for modernization of Korea by means of political education. They published Korea's first modern newspaper, the bilingual *Tongnip sinmun/Independent*, in which they criticized the government for selling out to foreign powers. Editorially and in public speeches they emphasized the spirit of freedom, civil rights, and national independence. Although the Independence Club existed for only a year, it was the first example of a democratic organization at work in Korea. It served as training ground for many young political leaders,

Tongnipmun, the Independence Gate in Seoul. Erected on the spot where the Korean court had traditionally met the envoy from China, it marked Korea's new role as an equal in that relationship. It is a symbol of the beginning of the long quest for independence of modern Korea. Hyungwon Kang

including Syngman Rhee, who was to become the first president of the Republic of Korea after World War II.

In 1897 King Kojong took the title of emperor, a symbolic attempt to equalize his position with that of the three emperors of China, Japan, and Russia. In the past the Korean king had been subordinate to the Chinese emperor; now he was to assume equal status, in title at least.

The following seven years were a relatively quiet period politically. Russia and Japan continued to vie for power on the peninsula, and foreign interests in Korea expanded. New ports were opened to trade, telegraphic communications were established, and an electric company began providing power to Seoul. The railway between Seoul and Inch'ŏn began operations, and in 1903 the first telephones came into use. Schools and hospitals were opened. The Protestant missionaries, who had been active since the opening of Korea in 1882, expanded their work greatly in one of the most successful undertakings in the history of Christian missions.

Then in 1904 Japan broke off diplomatic relations with Russia and, without a formal declaration of war, launched an attack on Russia. Most of the battles were fought outside Korean territory, but Korea was forced into the position of being Japan's ally. Japan won the Russo-Japanese War and assumed a place among the world's major powers. In the flush of victory the Japanese began to press their advantage in Korea.

In 1905 a Japanese-Korean agreement was signed, under strong Japanese pressure, establishing Korea as a Japanese protectorate. It gave the senior Japanese administrator, the Resident-General, complete power in the direction of Korean foreign relations, which were to be carried on through Tokyo.

The Resident-General's powers touched all fields of Korean governmental activity. The treaty was signed in secret, but secrets of that sort are hard kept, and as soon as the news became public, there were protests all over the peninsula. Some high-ranking court officials protested by committing suicide before the palace gates, and 1906 saw provincial revolts. But in the end, Japanese troops suppressed them all.

In 1906 all Korean foreign diplomatic missions were closed, and all foreign diplomatic missions in Korea withdrew in tacit acceptance of the Japanese right to control the peninsula. In 1907 the Korean emperor made his last move in the fight for Korean freedom from Japan. He secretly dispatched a delegation to the Second International Peace Conference at The Hague to plead Korea's cause. It met with no success, and one of the delegates, Yi Chun, committed suicide in protest. His grave in The Hague is a point of pilgrimage for all Koreans visiting Europe, and his life and death have been glamorized by a North Korean film.

That same year the emperor was forced by the Japanese to abdicate in favor of the crown prince, who they felt could be more easily controlled. In August 1910 a treaty of annexation was signed. Korea was incorporated into the Japanese empire. The Chosŏn Kingdom, founded by Yi Sŏng-gye, came to an end.

The Ferment of Cultures

After 1882 new cultural influences began to enter into Korea, especially from the West. In this process, usually called modernization, traditional values and beliefs came into contact with the often widely different values and beliefs of Western—that is, European and American—culture.

Before the opening of Korea to the West in 1882, there had been little significant contact with Protestant Christianity. The Roman Catholic priests had carried on their hidden work even with repeated persecutions, brought on in part by the Christian insistence that believers stop their ancestor worship and in part by the conservative fear of any foreign influence. There were an estimated twenty thousand Catholic Christians in Korea by the middle of the nineteenth century. It was only by terms of the 1882 treaty with the United States that Protestant missionaries were allowed to begin their work in Korea.

Linked with the new religions was the culture and learning of the West of which they were a part. The missionaries were quick to discover that schools were one of the most effective means of making lasting contact with young Koreans. Christianity in Korea is linked to the development of schools to teach Western science, languages, and medicine. Even today several major universities maintain ties and derive support from mission organizations and missionaries in the field. Western learning and Christianity, or Western religion, have been closely linked in Korean minds.

Korea accepted Christianity during the nineteenth century in a way no other East Asian nation has, and Christian churches continue to flourish. The Yoido Full Gospel Church, largest in Korea, and one of the largest in the world, boasts a congregation of half a million regular church-goers. Hyungwon Kang

In the transition, many of Korea's traditional literary and artistic forms were either totally changed or lost. In literature, for example, while many of the mask plays are still performed, and people still write *sijo*, they seem somehow old-fashioned. With the opening of Korea to the West in 1882, a new era had been ushered in. Korean writers began to look toward Western literature for their forms. When hymns and Western songs and melodies came to Korea with the missionaries near the end of the nineteenth century, Western musical and poetic forms also became popular. From this mixture were to come some of the first "modern" poems, the beginnings of another search for the proper balance between the traditional and the new.

The first modern poems were formed out of the meters of Christian hymns as translated into Korean and the fervor of love of country and the zeal for reform. Called simply "patriotic songs," they first appeared in *The Independent*, the newspaper published by Philip Jaisohn.

A fairly typical poem by a man named Yi Chung-wŏn, who does not seem to have published anything else, appeared in 1896. It draws together all the new themes: the awakening from the sleep of isolation, the reality of contact with the rest of the world, the importance of virtuous conduct, and above all, the need for a practical approach to the problems of the day.

> *Wake up from your sleep, wake up;*
> *This dream is four thousand years old.*
>
> *All the countries meet together,*
> *All the seas as in one family.*
>
> *Cast off all minor differences*
> *And uphold virtue with one mind.*
>
> *Why should we envy richer countries*
> *And make a virtue of poverty?*

We draw a dog looking at a tiger
And a hen gazing at the great auk.

If we are to be civilized, modernized,
Practical things must come first.

Let us not hope for a whale,
But be satisfied with minnows instead.

Though the net be hard to mesh,
Let us weave it with united purpose.

Korea was weak: The government could not govern; the tax monies went into the pockets of the collectors rather than into the treasury; foreign countries were draining the natural wealth of the mountains and plains. The Japanese, whom Koreans had for centuries thought of as uncivilized barbarians, were rapidly taking total control of the peninsula. The young nationalist, poet, and historian Ch'oe Nam-sŏn summed up the situation in 1909 in a poem, one of the first true literary works in the "new style":

One of the bands of the Righteous Armies in 1907. Farmers and members of the old Korean army, which had been disbanded by the Japanese, continued the fight against Japan from the countryside. Korean Cultural Center

We Have Nothing

We have nothing,
Neither sword nor pistol,
But we do not fear.
Even the might of the iron rule
Cannot move us.
We shoulder righteousness
And walk the path.

We have nothing to call our own,
Neither dagger nor powder,
But we do not fear.
Even with the power of the crown
They cannot move us.
Righteousness is the spade
With which we keep the main path.

We have nothing to hold in our hands,
Neither stone nor club,
But we do not fear.
All the wealth in this world
Cannot move us.
Righteousness is the sword
With which we guard the broad path.

But righteousness would not be enough. For forty years the iron hand of Japanese colonial rule squeezed the peninsula tight.

CHAPTER X

Korea in Our Century: *Chosen*/Japanese Colony

No Rising Sun [the Japanese flag] is hoisted by Koreans at their doors on national [that is, Japanese] holidays. This is a fact and a very unpleasant fact to Japanese. Mr. Shakuo, Editor of the Chosen and Manchuria, *a Japanese monthly published in Seoul, takes up the subject for discussion in its latest issue. . . . He considers it an act of traitors, reflecting contempt on the prestige of the Japanese Empire, and advocates the infliction of punishment by fines and flogging to all Koreans refusing to hoist the [Japanese] national flag on national holidays.*

Seoul Times, October 7, 1919

From 1910 to 1945 Korea remained a colony of Japan. This was a bitter experience. The stated aim of the Japanese in Korea was no less than the complete assimilation of a great and ancient nation and culture. During the first ten years, their rule was highly oppressive. Small local Korean "armies" offered armed resistance but were forced to retreat to

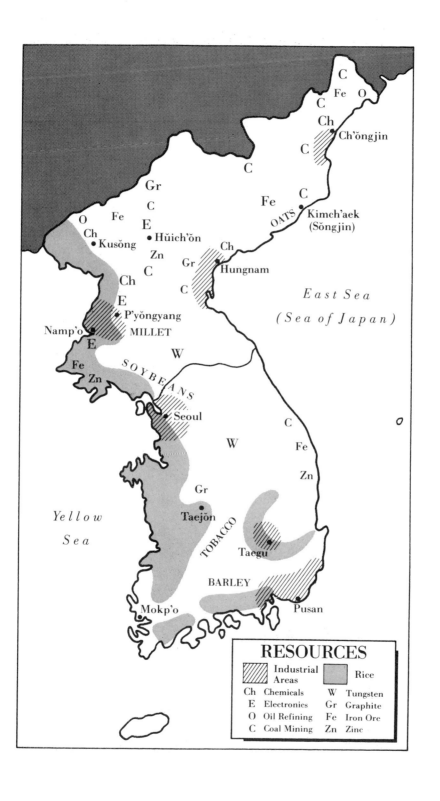

C
Fe O
C
Ch
● Ch'ŏngjin
C

Gr
C Fe
E C
O Fe OATS C
Ch
● Hŭich'ŏn Kimch'aek
Kusŏng Zn (Sŏngjin)
C
Ch Gr Ch
E C ● Hungnam
● P'yŏngyang
Namp'o ● MILLET
E East Sea
Fe W (Sea of Japan)
Zn SOYBEANS

● Seoul
W
C
Fe
Zn

Yellow Gr
Sea ● Taejŏn
TOBACCO
● Taegu
BARLEY
● Mokp'o ● Pusan

RESONRCES — *RESOURCES*

▨	Industrial Areas	▩ Rice

Ch Chemicals   W Tungsten
E Electronics   Gr Graphite
O Oil Refining   Fe Iron Ore
C Coal Mining   Zn Zinc

Manchuria by the overwhelming strength of the Japanese. Quick to gain control of land and the fledgling Korean industries, the Japanese developed transportation, fisheries, and communications, and exploited natural resources such as minerals and forests.

When the Japanese pointed with pride to their accomplishments on the peninsula, the Koreans asked: At what cost? What price do we Koreans have to pay to keep our rice pots filled? As Ch'oe Nam-sŏn put it in the 1920's:

To the Koreans mountains are not property to be bought and sold. Mountains are the precious ornaments of our land. They are where we exercise our minds and bodies; they are a symbol of the beliefs and ideals informing men and girls, individuals and communities, the life of now and the life of ideals. . . . Our Korean people as yet cannot think of filling their rice pots by selling them.

In actuality they had no choice. The Japanese had taken the mountains and everything else besides. But there was resistance. On March 1, 1919, there were peaceful demonstrations in Seoul demanding independence from Japan; within a few days the whole peninsula was in turmoil.

Despite tight censorship in Korea, the news spread, and soon the outside world was registering horror at the extent of Japanese brutalities. Pressures from world opinion demanded a change. In August 1919 the Governor-General was replaced.

Japanese power in the peninsula was not broken. But during the next decade the administration of that power was to be a little less severe. Japan had been forced to come to terms with the power of Korean national feeling.

But, while things were somewhat better for the next fifteen years, they were not good. In 1926, and again in 1928, there were student

March First Independence Movement

On March 1, 1919, a group of thirty prominent Koreans met around noon in a Seoul restaurant. They sent the Governor-General the Declaration of Independence that they had signed, as had three others who were not present. Then they called the Japanese police, explaining what they had done, and waited. By the time the police arrived to arrest them, the streets were lined with people cheering them as they went on their way to jail.

The Korean people were well aware of what was happening. By midafternoon special messengers had read the Declaration of Independence aloud in towns and villages all over the country. Peaceful demonstrations were held across the nation.

The timing of the March First Independence Movement was influenced by two events. The former Korean emperor had died and his funeral was scheduled for March 3. Common report had it that he had been poisoned by the Japanese, and resentment was at a boiling point. At the same time, America's President Woodrow Wilson's doctrine of self-determination for conquered nations was gaining strength around the world. Driven by this hope, a group of Korean students in Tokyo had published in February 1919 a statement demanding Korea's independence from Japan. By the first of March, plans had been made to reinforce this demand in Korea by means of peaceful demonstrations and the presentation of the Declaration of Independence to the Governor-General.

The demonstrations were peaceful, but the Japanese power retaliated in full force. There were wholesale imprisonments, open floggings, and brutal killings of demonstrators.

Japanese teacher in a Korean classroom during the occupation. The blackboard text, the pledge of allegiance to the Japanese emperor, is in mixed Chinese characters and Japanese hiragana *script.* Korean Cultural Center

uprisings against the Japanese. In 1929 nationwide anti-Japanese demonstrations occurred. In 1931, as Japan moved into Manchuria and toward war with China, controls became more rigid, and this continued during the 1930's. In 1936 a Korean marathon champion was able to enter the Olympic competition only by adopting a Japanese name and running as a representative of Japan. In 1938 the use of the Korean language in the schools was banned, along with the teaching of Korean history. In 1940 Koreans were ordered to adopt Japanese names. In the same year the two remaining Korean-language newspapers were suspended, and restrictions on all publications in Korean became most severe.

Korea had become an integral part of the Japanese war machine, and after the attack on Pearl Harbor in December of 1941 and the entry of the United States into World War II, Koreans were drafted wholesale into the Japanese army. Korea was stripped of anything that could be used to further the war effort: Workers went to factories in Japan, forests were leveled, even the iron pipes of the Seoul water system went to the iron-hungry blast furnaces.

The Fate of the Arts

It was the fate of Korean literature, and along with it the other arts, that early experiments with new styles were cut off by tight Japanese control of the press, the schools, and all media of expression. For many of the forty years of Japanese control, it was a dangerous thing to write in Korean. Because the Japanese hoped to replace Korean with Japanese as the language of the land, when a writer persisted in writing in Korean, particularly in the late 1930's and early 1940's, he or she was immediately suspected of holding anti-Japanese feelings. And indeed, writing in Korean was a way of affirming oneself as a Korean against the cultural aggression of the Japanese. From 1910 to 1945 Korean literature was in good part an expression of Korean national feeling, a way of saying, "I am a Korean no matter what." But it was a hard time, and often the poetry and prose reflected that.

Sim Hun's 1927 poem "Dirge" describes a funeral procession where the pallbearers making their way through the rain are dogged by the persistent Japanese detective:

> *We friends, biting hard on our lips,*
> *Heads bowed, trudging heavily on; no other mourners,*
> *No lover, no relative even—only one tailing along,*

Dogging this procession to that other world.
Forbidden even a funeral dirge we living dead,
Bearing the coffin, splash; on across the Muhak ridge.

And in Yang Chu-dong's "I Hear the Train Whistle" the rain echoes the Japanese oppression that is forcing travelers to leave their country, their homeland:

In the night rain
I hear the whistle of a distant train,
A sharp shrill sound trailing off to the north,
North, north across the fields.

Where are they going, these travelers,
Packed in coaches through the night?
How many have said good-bye to their country,
Wandering souls filled with blighted hopes?

Exile and Independence

Emigration and exile was the only answer for hundreds of thousands of Koreans in those years of Japanese occupation. Over 100,000 fled to Siberian Russia, over 300,000 to Manchuria already by 1910, while some 6,000 to 7,000 made their way to Hawaii and the United States.

These exile communities were centers of anti-Japanese activities. They soon had their own schools, newspapers, and cultural centers; in Manchuria and Siberia they trained guerrilla armies, and in the United States they even made an abortive attempt at building an air force. The central passion of Koreans away from their homeland, even the students in Japan, was the liberation and freedom of their country.

The plight of the lonely exile—frightened, on the move, alone, far from home and family, caught at what must have seemed the very top of the world among the mountains and plateaus of Manchuria—was given voice by Yi Hwal in his 1940 poem "The Vertex":

> *Lashed by the bitter season's scourge,*
> *I'm driven at length to this north*
>
> *Where numb circuit and plateau merge.*
> *I stand upon the swordblade frost;*
>
> *I know not where to bend my knees,*
> *Nor where to lay my galled steps—*
>
> *Naught but to close my eyes and think*
> *Of winter as a steel rainbow.*
>
> Translation by Yi In-su

The Korean Provisional Government in Shanghai and the worldwide independence movement were formed by the exiles and their leaders, many of whom had fled after the March First Independence Movement. And out of that came, for better or for worse, the first leaders of a liberated Korea.

Haebang-Hu/ Liberation and War

It was the end of last October when I first unpacked my vagabond luggage in the confused streets of Seoul amidst the chorus of party strife—I hit you and you hit me—everybody's party beating down everybody else's party in pamphlets rolling down Chongno Street and from the mouths of beautiful girls in the twisted sounds of broken English. Cafes and taverns are multiplying.

The "liberated country." Of course, it was the home I had yearned for.

From Kim Kwang-ju (1910–   ), "The Silent Mind," around 1948

Korea was freed from forty years of Japanese rule when Japan surrendered to the Allied Forces on August 15, 1945. Liberation was a gift of the great powers, not the end result of the independence struggles on the part of Koreans at home and abroad.

Korea was again caught up in a power struggle not of its own making. This time it was the "cold war" between the Soviet Union and the West. After the shouting and celebrations had died down, it soon became clear that creation of a unified and independent Korea would be no easy task.

The Japanese surrender in Korea was to be accepted by Soviet forces north of the thirty-eighth parallel and by American forces to the south. The result was a Korea divided at the middle.

As soon as the Japanese surrender was official, Korean leaders both north and south set up what was called the Preparatory Association for Establishing the Nation. Administrative units were established from the lowest to the highest levels to assure a continuance of civil order after the Japanese police and administrators left.

The Soviet forces came into Korea accompanied by many well-trained Koreans who had lived in Siberian Russia or China during the Japanese occupation, some of whom had served in the Soviet armies during World War II, some of whom had been with Chinese Communist leader Mao Zedong in Yenan, and most of whom were fiercely devoted to the cause of world communism.

The American forces were accompanied by few Koreans and almost no interpreters trained in the Korean language. The Koreans were mainly those who had carried on the anti-Japanese struggle in the United States, and they had been out of contact with Korea for years. As a result of these differences in personnel, the two occupying forces were to treat the local Korean organizations in very different ways.

The Soviet forces in the north did not often involve themselves directly in political developments. They left this up to their Russian-trained Korean fellows. Soon control of the Preparatory Association was in the hands of Koreans sympathetic to communism.

United States occupation forces set up a military government in the south. To many in South Korea it seemed as if they had simply exchanged one foreign rule for another. And to make the situation worse, their country was now divided.

Despite joint efforts by the Soviet Union, the United States, and Britain to work out the problems of unification, the situation remained deadlocked until, in 1947, the United States placed the Korean question before the second session of the United Nations General Assembly. A United Nations Temporary Commission for Korea was set up to supervise general elections over the whole of the peninsula. When the commission tried to carry out the planned elections, it found itself barred from the Soviet-occupied zone in the north.

In 1948 general elections under United Nations supervision were carried out in the south only. The party led by Syngman Rhee—a man who had devoted his life to the cause of Korean independence but who had spent the forty years of the occupation in the United States—won the elections after a period of bitter fighting among the many political groups seeking power. He was the first president of the Republic of Korea. This government was recognized by the United Nations as the only legitimate government of all Korea.

The Korean Democratic People's Republic was set up in the north with its capital at P'yŏngyang, and the division of Korea was complete. This government was led by Kim Il Sung, a Korean Communist general who was claimed to have led a guerrilla army in Manchuria during the 1930's. By 1950 most hopes for peaceful unification of the country under one government had been lost. On June 25, 1950, war broke out along the thirty-eighth parallel.

The North Korean forces advanced rapidly, taking Seoul and bottling up the South Korean forces in the area around Pusan on the southern tip of the peninsula. It was at this point that President Truman ordered American forces into Korea to assist the South Korean army.

On June 27, the United Nations recommended that its members support the South Koreans against the aggression from the north. The United Nations Command was set up in Korea in July, and as the war progressed, the forces of sixteen nations were fighting in Korea. Seven other nations sent hospital ships, field hospitals, and other assistance.

Mini Facts

The Republic of Korea

POPULATION: 42,380,000 (1989)

DENSITY: 1,104 persons per square mile (427 per square kilometer)

URBAN/RURAL: 69 percent urban, 31 percent rural

EDUCATION: Adult literacy rate at 92.7 percent in 1980; primary school education is universal and compulsory (grades 1 through 6), but nearly all students complete secondary (age 19) and about half continue on to either vocational or university training

HEALTH: Dramatic improvement in health conditions since 1960's; health personnel and facilities tremendously expanded

LIFE EXPECTANCY: Men, 70 years; women, 73 years (1986)

LANGUAGE: Korean

RELIGION: Buddhism, Confucianism, and Catholic and Protestant Christianity; also as many as 300 new religions that incorporate Buddhist, Confucianist, and Christian elements, principal among them Ch'ŏndogyo; shamanistic rites still common today

ECONOMY

GENERAL CHARACTER: Rapidly industrializing, middle-income country with dynamic export sector

AGRICULTURE, FORESTRY, AND FISHING: Major crops: rice, barley, fruits, and vegetables; livestock and dairy products increasingly important; fish products popular food and important export commodity; forestry reserves inadequate

INDUSTRY: Main growth sector, including trade. Produced nearly 64% of gross national product

IMPORTS: $31.6 billion (U.S. equivalent), 1986; major imports were machinery and transport equipment, mineral fuels, raw materials for manufacturing, and chemicals and chemical products

EXPORTS: $34.7 billion, 1986; major commodities: textiles, iron and steel, electronic equipment, and machinery; construction services and tourist industry also major foreign-exchange earners

MAJOR TRADE AREAS: Japan, United States, European Community member states, Middle East, and Southeast Asia; markets in Latin America and Africa opening more slowly

TRANSPORTATION: Roads: 32,475 miles (52,654 kilometers), half of which paved. Railroads: 3,914 miles (6,299 kilometers) of track. Ports and airfields: two large, ten major, and sixteen minor ports; two international airports and domestic service between eight principal cities

COMMUNICATIONS: Domestic and international communications under supervision of Ministry of Communications; no restrictions on radio or television reception; radios are common, one for every three persons. One television for every two or three persons; one telephone for every six persons; seven daily newspapers and hundreds of periodicals

GOVERNMENT AND POLITICS

POLITICAL SYSTEM: Multiparty republic with a national assembly; in 1988 President Roh Tae Woo elected by direct vote in first peaceful transfer of power since government established in 1948

ADMINISTRATIVE DIVISIONS: Four provincial-level special cities (Seoul, Pusan, Taegu, and Inch'ŏn) and nine provinces

LEGAL SYSTEM: Supreme Court tops three-level court system; high courts in middle; district courts and their branches at bottom

FOREIGN AFFAIRS: Member of most international organizations but no formal membership yet in United Nations; mutual defense treaty with United States, which, along with Japan, is one of two most important foreign policy partners

NATIONAL SECURITY

ARMED FORCES: Total personnel on active duty about 629,000

INTERNAL SECURITY FORCES: National Police totals approximately 50,000, organized under the Ministry of Home Affairs; other internal security forces are Agency for National Security Planning and Defense Security Command

The war continued up and down the length of the peninsula for over two years. After the formation of the United Nations Command in July 1950, the North Korean forces were slowly pushed north until, at the end of October, United Nations forces were at the Yalu River on the Manchurian border.

At this point, troops from mainland China entered the war, again forcing a retreat south of Seoul by the South Korean and United Nations forces. By the end of March 1951, the South Korean and United Nations troops had forced their way back to the thirty-eighth parallel. Two months later, a fairly stable battle line had been established in the general area of the parallel. Truce talks began in July 1951.

After two years of negotiations an armistice agreement was finally reached. Peace of a sort came to Korea when it was signed on July 27, 1953. A military demarcation line was established along the front where fighting had been taking place during the long months of negotiation. A distance of two kilometers on either side of this line was designated a no-man's-land, known as the Demilitarized Zone, or DMZ.

The years that followed were not easy ones. There was the agonizing realization that the division of the country was to continue. Both north and south were faced with the problems of rebuilding out of the destruction of war.

Taehan Min'guk/The Republic of Korea

The proper relation between king and people was severed by democracy. The amicable relation between father and son was cut by the 38th parallel. The distinction between husband and wife was chopped off by the liberation. The proper order between aged and young was cut by the call of "comrade." Sincerity between friends was severed by ideologies. We have this kind of joke.

Kim Sŏng-jin, 1905–

The Republic of Korea was created on May 10, 1948. A national assembly was elected that approved a constitutional government patterned on that of the United States. On August 15, 1948, General Douglas MacArthur, as commander of United States forces in the Far East, turned over the United States military government in Korea to the first president of the independent Republic of Korea, Syngman Rhee.

The Rhee Years

Syngman Rhee had been a junior member of the Independence Club and active in efforts to liberalize the Korean monarchy. Imprisoned and

The Hunters Are Beating
the Streets of Seoul

The use of goon squads as hit men was commonplace in the years
when Rhee was consolidating his power. Seoul was not a safe place
for those with dissident political views. Sŏl Chong-sik, in his poem
"Seoul," likened it to the mountains during hunting season.

> *The hunters are beating*
> *the streets of Seoul*
> *where there are no hills or valleys.*
>
> *Mayday, with plenty of spring shoots,*
> *they have stolen our fatherland.*
>
> *Mayday,*
> *just before the peony falls*
>
> *that day*
> *has been youth's day to learn death;*

tortured by both his own government and later the Japanese, after
release he made his way to Japan, Hawaii, and eventually the mainland
United States. After completing studies at Princeton, he returned to
Korea as a YMCA worker. He, like many of the South Korean political
leaders of that time, was a Christian. Soon after the annexation he left
Korea again for Hawaii.

During his years of exile, Rhee worked continuously for the cause of
Korean independence. When he returned to Korea at the end of the
Pacific war—after living abroad for the greater part of forty years—he
was already past seventy.

the day
to learn death like wrestling.

Just before the peony fell
the young fighters,
their sides rent,
took one step more, then fell.

Sŏl Chong-sik had been educated at an American university during the Japanese occupation years at least in part through the help of an American missionary family with whom he had lived as he was growing up, friend and playmate to their sons.

He ultimately turned North, and five years after publishing this poem, while serving as interpreter for the North at the P'anmunjŏm truce negotiations, he was face to face across the table with a childhood friend and companion, the son of the American missionary family with whom he had lived not so long before. He died soon after, his broken health saving him some of the breaking of the spirit that came to others in the purges of 1953.

Syngman Rhee created intense loyalties and violent opposition. He was careful not to allow any opposing politician to grow too strong; he did not hesitate to cut down members of his own party if he felt they were gaining too much popularity. His followers resorted to political assassination in the process of consolidating and holding power. In the end, his government became dictatorial, suppressing democratic processes and civil liberties.

The older Rhee grew, the more isolated he became from the real political needs of the nation he had loved so passionately; many pressing needs of the nation were being neglected.

Rhee's was a "strongman" government. When conflicts occurred within the three branches of government, the president most often emerged with the real power. Rhee, a skillful and ruthless politician, forced through several constitutional amendments strengthening presidential powers, yet for years managed to preserve the appearance of respecting democratic processes and organizations.

Violently anti-Japanese to the end, Rhee allowed no easing of tensions with Japan while he was in power. He was conservative, politically and personally, committed to a program of reunifying the peninsula by force, and given to calling anyone he didn't like a Communist, whether it was true or not.

Still, in a time of great crises, during the years of the Korean War, Syngman Rhee served as a popular rallying point for the defense of the South. The first titular and real leader of well over half the Korean people after forty years of colonial rule, he continued as president of the Republic of Korea until his government was overthrown by student demonstrations in April 1960.

A Parliamentary Interlude

In July 1960 elections were held. A parliamentary form of government was established with Yun Po Sun as president and John M. Chang as premier. The new government brought an interlude of unprecedented gaiety and spontaneity to everyday life. But living conditions were getting worse, not better. John Chang turned out to be an ineffectual leader.

The police had been so thoroughly discredited that even newly organized, and with full government support, they found it difficult to maintain civil order. For the first time since 1948 the government, while maintaining a strong anticommunist stance, renounced military means as the only way to reunification. Greater freedom of the press led to open talk of reconciliation with the north, rank heresy in Rhee days and, in the eyes of many, even then. There were protest demonstrations everywhere and against everything.

The economy faltered badly; inflation was severe. Little was done, though much was said, about a new agricultural program. A black market, reminiscent of the days shortly after the Korean War, flourished.

In the early morning hours of May 16, 1961, a group of Korean soldiers took control of government buildings, the radio stations, and the city of Seoul in a bloodless coup. The gaiety ended, and the streets of the city were lined with Koreans young and old, their impassive faces watching the passing military convoys. After years of repressions and hopes, and more repressions, and hopes rekindled, most South Koreans could feel only emotional exhaustion and submission to fate.

The Park Years: Government

Under the military, a governing body of thirty-two officers called the Supreme Council for National Reconstruction led the nation. President Yun Po Sun was retained in office to give some semblance of constitutional continuity. The Supreme Council quickly set about writing a new constitution.

Not too many weeks passed before Major General Park Chung Hee emerged as the strongman of the military government, which then moved toward immediate reforms in major problem areas. They struck out first at graft and political corruption. All political activities were suspended; people who had amassed large fortunes through alleged corrupt or illegal means were forced to donate large sums to national economic projects or to pay heavy fines. The press was muzzled, the government said, to stop the publication of "irresponsible papers," but the censor's hand reached much further than that.

Despite a promise of early elections and a return to civilian rule, the Supreme Council, zealous for reform, seemed to think the country could be run like an army. But they soon found that the needs of civilians, and the economic and political problems of running a country, require solutions very different from simple military orders or decrees.

In elections held in 1963, Park Chung Hee ran as a civilian and won by a small margin. There was no reason to question the fairness of the elections. The presidential election was followed by elections for the legislature, and again President Park's Democratic-Republican Party carried a majority. The Republic of Korea was once again under presumably civilian rule, though most important positions were filled by former military officers.

President Park and those around him were practical men. They knew very well how much the Republic of Korea depended upon U.S. and other foreign aid. Yet he and his advisors believed it was most important that Koreans find Korean solutions to Korean problems, even though in so doing they might have to rely heavily upon foreign models. The model they chose was one of strong central government control of economic and industrial planning. This was set out in the economic plan for 1962 to 1969, which was drawn up to deal with a too rapidly growing population, a static economy, and rapid inflation.

In the face of the instability and unrest in South Korea brought on by the difficult economic situation came greater and greater repressions: suppression of civil rights, press censorship, the brutality of an unchecked civilian police and military intelligence apparatus. It was a military reaction rather than a political one to a political problem.

Crucial to the economic plan was establishing diplomatic and trade relations with Japan and as many friendly nations as possible. One legacy of the Rhee years that stood in the way was a younger generation of students who had grown up hating the Japan they knew from their textbooks as the former brutal colonial power. Yet without diplomatic and trade relations with Japan, South Korea was almost totally dependent upon the United States, which granted it special favors as trading partner. Open negotiations for a treaty were begun in March of 1964, and by April students began demonstrations. By the time the treaty was ready to be signed in June of 1965, martial law had been declared.

For each step gained in economic growth or international contacts, more restrictions were put on civil liberties. The press was stifled; poets, students, and protesters were jailed. It is against this backdrop of excessive repression and tight central planning that South Korea's economic growth must be evaluated. The South Korean "miracle" is not really testament to a free economy. Rather, it is a question of what a people is willing, or needs, to give up to achieve a place in the modern world.

The Park Years: Economic Growth

With the signing of a treaty with Japan in June of 1965 that established full diplomatic recognition for South Korea, but not North, South Korea entered into a new period of economic growth. The treaty had among its provisions a $500-million aid program. With a new economic policy concentrating on overseas exports, this new capital gave the economy a much-needed boost.

In the 1960's the Republic of Korea remained an agricultural economy, though exports and manufacturing were becoming more and more important. Hard work and tremendous sacrifice on the part of the Korean people, careful planning and strict enforcement on the part of the South Korean government, growth of trade with Japan, most favored

Hopes for Reunification

One of the most exciting developments during the Park years was the new openness and hopes for negotiations toward a peaceful reunification of Korea. But at the end of 1971 prospects looked very poor indeed. President Park had proclaimed a state of national emergency on December 6, in view of the changing international scene, including the entry of Communist China into the United

The Korean War was fought, from the South, as a United Nations peacekeeping effort; and the military in the South, including U.S. troops, were under a U.N. military command. Here the North Korean delegates at P'anmunjŏm face their U.N. counterparts across the table to discuss a truce violation.   Hyungwon Kang

Nations and the "fanatic war preparations being carried out by the Communist regime in North Korea."

At the time, this appeared to mark an end to the talks proposed by the Red Cross organizations of both North and South Korea in August 1971, but the Red Cross negotiations continued, culminating with the establishment of a formal agenda and an agreement to hold meetings alternately in the capitals of the two halves of the peninsula. The South Korean delegation first visited P'yŏngyang in August 1972, and the North Korean delegation was greeted by cheering crowds in Seoul on September 13, 1972.

For the first time in nearly thirty years, the wall of the Demilitarized Zone had been broached by other than intelligence agents and provocateurs.

By February of 1973 the talks had been broken off again, and in the following years, while communications at least remain open, the hopes for real negotions have been lost in the maneuvering for political and diplomatic position by both North and South.

In the spring of 1985 proposals were made for an exchange of visits by family members from the North and the South, and agreement was made for an exchange of home visits and art troupes. From September 20 to 23, 1985, groups of hometown visitors and art troupes were exchanged between Seoul and P'yŏngyang via P'anmunjŏm.

As 1990 drew to an end there were renewed, if cautious, hopes that negotiations were beginning to work. There had been North-South exchanges of soccer teams, musicians, and performers, and each Premier had visited the other's capital. There seemed finally to be a substantive beginning down the long, slow road of negotiations that ultimately would lead to peaceful reunification.

Very early in the industrialization process South Korea started to emphasize heavy industry. Today the Republic of Korea has some of the most modern iron and steel manufacturing facilities in the world, such as this Posco steel plant in Kyangyang.
Hyungwon Kang

treatment as a trading partner by the United States—all played a part in the advances made under the 1967 to 1971 Second Economic Development Plan.

Industry

The treaty with Japan in 1965 provided a source of aid to growing industry in Korea, as well as a market for Japanese goods in Korea and Korean goods in Japan. But no amount of money will do an industrializing nation any good unless there is some way to use it.

The Republic of Korea was fortunate in having a well-educated labor force with managerial and high technological skills and a large population available for unskilled labor. A good part of South Korea's success in industrialization was due to the employment of young, single women in the work force.

By the late 1970's the Republic of Korea was no longer receiving aid; a normal trade relationship had been established with both the United States and Japan, as well as with many other Western countries. Many foreign businesses invested in manufacturing plants in Korea because of the cheap and highly efficient labor. In the mid-1960's in one year alone more than fifty large plants were opened in South Korea with investment from not only the United States and Japan, but also West Germany, France, Britain, and others.

At the same time, the government kept a close eye on what was going on. Intensive development was targeted for manufacturing industries such as machinery, shipbuilding, chemicals, and steel. Since these were all products that the South Koreans would have to import if they did not manufacture them themselves, development in these areas served not only to increase exports, but to meet home needs as well.

Agriculture: *Saemaŭl undong / The New Community Movement*   As industry prospered, the rural villages were not going anywhere. Poverty was the rule in the villages, and there seemed no way out. Then a program of revitalization was launched from the highest level, the presidential office.

Dependent on the Korean farmers' own capacity for hard cooperative labor, the Saemaŭl Movement brought the farmers up to the level of industrial workers in a short time.

Beginning with pilot projects in 1970, the government provided simple help, such as cement for new roads and bridges. Thatched roofs were replaced by tile. Wells were cleaned up and water supplies enclosed. Ox paths were replaced by concrete roads. Electricity, radio, and television are now commonplace.

But a better gauge of the improvements in agriculture is the simple

The modernization and mechanization of agriculture have not been completed. Here a farmer tills his paddy with an ox and hand-guided plow in Koch'ang, North Chŏlla Province. The new metal-roofed home in the background stands beside the former "grass" or thatched-roof one. Hyungwon Kang

fact that by the late 1970's South Korea was self-sufficient in rice and barley production, whereas a few years earlier both rice and barley had been major imports from the United States.

President by Decree

After his reelection by a narrow margin in December 1971 and under provisions of the new Yusin (Revitalization) Constitution of December 1972, which gave the president extraordinary powers, Park began to act much like a dictator. The new constitution allowed the president to take emergency measures pretty much as he pleased. It also weakened the powers of the parliament and changed the method of selecting presidents from a popular vote to voting by members of a select body.

Red Cross talks were opened with North Korea in 1972. But by the spring of 1973 they had been broken off, and a period of North Korean aggression began.

The final years of Park Chung Hee's presidency were violent. In 1974 his wife was assassinated by a North Korean agent, as Park made a speech proposing new initiatives for reunification. In 1974 and 1975, and later in 1978, North Korean tunnels under the Demilitarized Zone were discovered, all of which gave the government more excuses for emergency decrees.

Park was reelected under the Yusin Constitution to another six-year term in 1978. In 1979 violent student demonstrations broke out in Pusan and other southern cities. On October 25 President Park was assassinated. A new president was elected on December 6, only to be faced with a December 12 coup engineered and led by General Chun Doo Hwan.

The following year, 1980, saw the Republic of Korea tormented as it had not been since the war. Mass student demonstrations against the repressive government began in May. An emergency decree was issued banning all political activities and dissolving all political parties. From May 19 to 22, some 200,000 citizens and students clashed with military forces in Kwangju. They took over government offices and seized police stations and armories.

On May 22 paratroopers were brought in. They stormed the city and restored order at the cost of hundreds of deaths and thousands of wounded—a bloody and unnecessary tragedy in a land that had already seen too much bloodshed.

On the ninth anniversary of the Kwangju uprising, families of the victims of army brutality mourn their dead at the Mangwŏldong Cemetery in Kwangju. Hyungwon Kang

It was at this point that General Chun made a call for new leaders to build a democratic society. He insisted, as had Park Chung Hee before him, that the nation could make no progress without out cleaning up the mess of corruption that characterized the government. And like Park before him, Chun took off his uniform and was elected president.

The Chun presidency was to last until 1988. He had cleaned up the corruption of the preceding government only to be tangled in that of his own. But he had made another promise, perhaps more important in the long run, which was that there would be a peaceful transfer of power after regular elections.

While it took widespread protests and disruptions by students widely supported by the middle class to force popular elections, they were held and Roh Tae Woo was elected president just before Seoul was to host

Continuous demonstrations in 1987, like this one in downtown Seoul in which college students were joined by ordinary citizens, led to the political reforms that allowed a direct presidential election.   Hyungwon Kang

Seoul National University students take to the streets in a call for the reunification of North and South Korea, 1988.   Hyungwon Kang

A middle-aged woman berates the riot police in front of the Myŏngdong Catholic Cathedral in downtown Seoul, in June 1987.   Hyungwon Kang

It was the pressure of student demonstrations joined by an increasingly dissatisfied citizenry that led to a direct presidential election in 1987. Here students in Seoul keep up that pressure calling for a "fair" election during the campaign.   Hyungwon Kang

Free and fair elections do not always go smoothly. Here a ruling-party rally turned into a riot. Chŏnju, North Chŏlla Province, 1987.   Hyungwon Kang

In South Korea dissent often landed a person in prison. Here the families of political prisioners demonstrate in downtown Seoul calling for their release.   Hyungwon Kang

The 1987 elections in the South marked the first in which there was direct election of the president in seventeen years. The people responded enthusiastically. Here over a million

persons are gathered in Yoido Plaza for a speech by Kim Dae Jong, a major opposition leader. Hyungwon Kang

the 1988 Olympic games. This was a triumphant moment for South Korea. Visitors came from around the world; a democratically elected government was in place; the games went off without major problems and, most importantly, without a boycott by the Eastern bloc nations in support of North Korea's decision not to participate.

The result has been that the Republic of Korea now has trade and diplomatic doors opened across the world that had been closed before.

CHAPTER XIII

Chosŏn Minjujuŭi Inmin Konghwaguk/ The Democratic People's Republic of Korea

Among the million peaks called the "Stubborn Million"
Is there one your feet did not touch?
Is there a valley your hands did not touch?
You took the barren soil rejected by all others
And nurtured it till the hill was golden as any plain.

Reading all the long night in a thatched hut,
Four cornerposts staked into the forbidding mountains,
You learned the true meaning of the party,
You extended the boundless strength of youth.

Yi Hyo-un's eulogy to a "party member"
killed by a train as he attempted to save a calf

The Making of a Communist State

The Democratic People's Republic of Korea came into being at the same time as the Republic of Korea. During the transition period from military control, the Communist Party was able to build a party structure on the system of committees that Koreans had already put into place to maintain civil order after the Japanese surrender. During the transition to local Korean control these "people's committees" were quickly brought under Communist Party control. Operating at county, city, and provincial levels, the committees in turn sent representatives who made up the Provisional North Korean People's Committee. This body unanimously elected Kim Il Sung chairman and drafted necessary legislation

A spectacular crag in the Diamond Mountains topped by a lone pine on the east coast of North Korea. Se Hoon Park/The Korea Times U.S.A.

for the operation of government, as well as adopting a draft constitution modeled on that of the Soviet Union.

National elections held in November 1946 presented the voters with a single slate of candidates who were to serve as delegates to a convention of the People's Committees.

The convention, held in February 1947, approved the legislation and constitution as presented by the Provisional People's Committee. They also elected the North Korean People's Assembly as the supreme legislative organ of the government. On the same day, February 21, the newly elected People's Assembly gave permanent status to the People's Committee and announced the formation of a twenty-man executive cabinet headed by Kim Il Sung.

While there have been turnovers and changes in the higher ranks of government since 1948, and a major purge in 1958, Kim Il Sung has retained his position as both head of state and head of the Korean Workers' (Communist) Party. The stability and continuity of North Korea have not been shaken by public internal dissent and military coup, as in the South. This is a stability brought by the rigid controls of the police state.

In December 1972 Kim Il Sung, as the only candidate, was elected president of the Democratic People's Republic of Korea under a new constitution, drafted so as to provide for a new era of coexistence leading to peaceful reunification with the Republic of Korea. In practice, though, North Korean policy seems to favor overthrow of the South through internal revolution. Both North and South Korea feel the weight of this potential for violence; both remain battle ready with high military expenditures.

There have been problems in maintaining party solidarity, but these problems have been to a large degree worked out within the highly secretive structure of the party itself; political problems are not put on public display as they are in the more open South.

The Korean Workers' Party grew out of three disparate groups: those who organized and worked in Korea itself during the Japanese occupation, those who were attached to Chinese Communist groups in Yenan in the 1930's and 1940's, and those who were centered in Manchuria and Siberia, many of them acting as guerrilla forces against the Japanese. In order to maintain his position, Kim Il Sung—who belonged to the Manchurian group and was Russian trained—dealt ruthlessly with the other two Communist groups as well as all other political organizations.

Two nominal opposition parties were allowed to function for a while, but soon became powerless. The struggle for power went on within the higher ranks of the Workers' Party itself, where Kim Il Sung first accommodated, then, as his power increased, got rid of, the more powerful members of rival Communist groups. In 1958 members of the Korean-based Communist Party were purged, that is, executed or removed from positions of power, and the constant shifting of those in high positions soon made it apparent that the old China-based Communists were losing their influence as well.

In the South the army, with its highly trained administrative personnel, ultimately proved the major threat to the government in power; in the North, at the end of the Korean War, the military leadership was purged. In this way Kim Il Sung was able to switch the blame for losing the war from his shoulders to those of the generals, while at the same time effectively removing a potentially threatening group from positions of power.

Kim Il Sung was seventy-eight in 1990. He has headed the Democratic People's Republic for more than half his life. A cult of the "people's hero," the "great and glorious leader," has been built around this architect of one of the last of the brutally repressive small Communist states, and perhaps the one about which the least is known.

Mini Facts

The Democratic People's Republic of Korea

SOCIETY

POPULATION: 22,418,000 (1989)

DENSITY: 474 persons per square mile (183 per square kilometer)

URBAN/RURAL: 64 percent urban; 36 percent rural

EDUCATION: Eleven-year compulsory education system, beginning with kindergarten at age six and ending with last year of Higher Middle School at age sixteen; less than 10 percent continue to university level; extensive system of adult and correspondence education; literacy, 90 percent

HEALTH: Hospitals and clinics with modern facilities throughout country; health care free to all citizens; strong emphasis placed on preventive medicine

LIFE EXPECTANCY: Men, 65 years; women, 72 years (1986)

LANGUAGE: Korean

RELIGION: Religious expression now largely suppressed

ECONOMY

GENERAL CHARACTER: Socialized, centralized, and planned economy

AGRICULTURE, FORESTRY, AND FISHING: Principal crops: rice, corn, coarse grains, pulses, and vegetables; livestock increasingly important; fishing and forestry receiving increased government investment and support; exports include rice, corn, apples, fish, and forestry products; wheat imports needed to meet domestic demand

INDUSTRY: Contributed over half of national income in 1980's

IMPORTS: Approximately $2 billion (U.S. equivalent), 1986; major imports are crude petroleum, coal, and coke; industrial machinery and transport equipment such as trucks; industrial chemicals; textile yarn and fabrics; and grain

EXPORTS: Approximately $1.7 billion, 1986. Major exports are semimanufactured metal products, magnesite powder, lead, zinc, and cement

MAJOR TRADE AREAS: U.S.S.R., People's Republic of China, and Japan

TRANSPORTATION: Complete reconstruction of system destroyed during Korean War, but lags behind needs of economy; total railway network of 2,779 miles (4,473 kilometers), mostly standard-gauge track, well over half electrified; 13,670 miles (22,000 kilometers) of roads, of which only 2 percent are paved; three airports with scheduled flights; port facilities are being constantly upgraded to expand international shipping

COMMUNICATIONS: Domestic and international communication controlled through Propaganda and Agitation Department of Communist Party; radio access from government networks; nearly every household has access to broadcasts from transistor radios (one per five persons) or public loudspeakers; television transmission widespread (one set per nineteen persons); telephones are few (one per 2,000 persons); eleven daily newspapers and a wide range of publications

GOVERNMENT AND POLITICS

POLITICAL SYSTEM: Communist state under leadership of Kim Il Sung, general secretary of ruling Korean Workers Party (KWP) and president of state

ADMINISTRATIVE DIVISIONS: Nine provinces and four provincial-level special cities, all under direct central control

LEGAL SYSTEM: Three-level judicial system patterned after Soviet model

FOREIGN AFFAIRS: Has been allied with Soviet Union, China, and other socialist countries; North Korea's foreign relations have focused on socialist countries, nonaligned nations, and newly emerging countries; maintains an observer mission to the United Nations and participates in many of its specialized agencies as well as those of other international organizations

NATIONAL SECURITY

ARMED FORCES: Armed forces, known collectively as Korean People's Army (KPA), total about 840,000

INTERNAL SECURITY FORCES: Internal security and maintenance of law and order centered in Ministry of Public Security; both conventional and secret police apparatus tightly controlled by Party

Economic Development

Under Kim Il Sung's leadership North Korea had made an impressive recovery even before the Korean War broke out. All industries had been nationalized and were beginning to function, though most military equipment and technical supplies had to be imported from Russia; and as in the South, huge quantities of outside aid were needed.

Major land reforms were instituted immediately. Farmers were given rights to the land they worked (though this did not entail ownership since these rights could not be sold, rented, or mortgaged). All large landholdings were broken up. Sweeping reforms were also undertaken in education, health, and welfare services—indeed, everything was geared to attainment of goals set by the government, and the education of the people to the government-espoused ideology and beliefs. Reforms were barely underway, however, when the Korean War wreaked almost total destruction upon industry and power supplies in the North. The city of P'yŏngyang was rubble at the end of the war.

In 1954 the Democratic People's Republic of Korea (D.P.R.K.) embarked upon a series of economic plans in an effort to restore destroyed industry. For the first ten years or so the greatest concentration was upon heavy industry: machine building, metallurgy, chemicals, and electric power. The required outside aid was found mostly in Eastern Europe. By 1963 the Democratic People's Republic claimed it had achieved basic industrial independence and would be able to continue internal industrial growth sustained by its own technological and economic resources. By 1967 it claimed more than ten times the industrial production of 1947.

North Korea was held up as an Asian showplace for communism, much as the rapid economic growth of the Republic of Korea in the late 1960's gained it the label of an Asian showplace for democracy. Today, however, the Democratic People's Republic is plagued by its inability to pay its foreign debt, and a chronic lack of foreign exchange and capital to develop further.

While there is no doubt that the Democratic People's Republic worked a remarkable recovery from the Korean War and established a firm industrial base in a very short time, the costs in human terms have been appalling. Today North Korea produces tractors, buses, and electric and diesel locomotives. There are oil refineries and steel and chemical plants. Machine tool plants produce nearly all the industrial equipment required for a relatively unsophisticated technology.

Less than half the population works in agriculture. Farms were collectivized between 1954 and 1958. There are no single-family farms, only cooperative farms, most of them large, averaging around twelve hundred acres and worked by about three hundred families. There are nearly four thousand of these farms with their irrigated fields, tractors, and electricity. Chemical fertilizers are in general use. Increased efficiency in farming methods has led to both an increase in agricultural production and less need for field labor. The surplus labor has been moved to industry, for unlike the South with its labor surplus, the North has been troubled with a chronic labor shortage. One result has been the appearance of women as equals of men in all kinds of work, from field labor to construction to the professions such as medicine. Another result has been the constant demand for more work from each laborer— longer and longer shifts with less and less time off in order to meet state-imposed production schedules and quotas.

An Isolated Nation

The Democratic People's Republic of Korea remains one of the most isolated nations in the world. Most reports by outside observers have been made by those sympathetic to the Communist regime and committed to its ends. Even now with the general easing of tensions in East Asia and the cataclysmic changes taking place in Eastern and Central Europe, there are no clear signs that North Korea's isolation is likely to come to an end. When foreign journalists or scholars visit, their movements are tightly controlled. There is no reporting of the underside of North Korea, as there is in the South. There has been in the past few years an increasing flow of Korean Americans and other overseas Koreans returning home to find family and friends and visit their childhood homes. Their accounts are more broadly based than most, but even their visits are closely restricted.

Impressions of the South are of noise and clamor, of constant human interactions, sometimes pleasant, sometimes jarring, but always personal. By contrast, Donald K. Chung, a Long Beach, California, cardiologist, whose autobiography *The Three Day Promise* describes a recent visit to his family home in the North, was struck by the coldness and impersonality of P'yŏngyang:

The streets of P'yŏngyang were immaculate, wide and clearly well-maintained, if a little underused. I was frankly surprised to see so many tall modern buildings rising above the beautiful tree-lined sidewalks. The main thing that struck me then, and throughout my stay in the capital, was the oppressive feeling of isolation from my fellow human beings. We saw few pedestrians and very, very few other cars. . . . P'yŏngyang had all the earmarks of a science-fiction city that had been abandoned in mid-beat by its entire population.

I could not stop the inevitable workings of my mind. This sterile cityscape reminded me of thoughts I had had over the weeks since [my sister's letter] about the utter control the government of North Korea had over its citizens. Where else in the world, I had asked myself, could one locate three married women after a thirty-year interval, and in so relatively short a time? I had long tried to imagine the infinite tentacles of such a government, but my life in the West had rendered me incapable of imagining the implications of such a thing.

Violence

From the signing of the Armistice at the end of the Korean War, the North has kept up a constant effort to undermine the governments in the South. On the other hand, the North sees the continued presence of U.S. troops in the South as a threat.

There has been a kind of dramatic violence in many of the aggressive moves on the part of the North. In January 1968, thirty-one North Korean armed commandoes were sent to Seoul with the mission of assassinating President Park. Three days later the North Koreans captured an American intelligence-gathering ship, the *USS Pueblo,* on the high seas. In November of 1968 thirty North Korean guerrillas landed on the east coast of the South. In September 1970 a North Korean agent was captured as he attempted to rig an explosive charge on a site where President Park was to appear the next day.

An unarmed South Korean fishing boat was sunk and another captured by North Korean naval craft in the Yellow Sea. In June 1980 South Korean naval craft sank an infiltrating armed North Korean spy boat off the west coast.

On October 9, 1983, while President Chun was on an official visit to Burma, a remote-controlled bomb planted by North Korean agents exploded at the Martyrs' Mausoleum in Rangoon, killing eighteen ranking South Korean officials and wounding fourteen others. In 1988, just prior to the Olympic Games in Seoul, North Korean agents in the Middle East planted a bomb in a Korean Airlines plane that exploded while over Burmese airspace, killing all on board.

One result of these continued acts of violence and terrorism has been an increased isolation of North Korea from the world community.

This speaks directly to the first of two things that need to be considered when measuring North Korea's accomplishments. First, and perhaps most important, has been the sterile, brooding stability of the North Korean government in contrast to the noisy, fruitful instability in the South. Kim Il Sung has retained power since 1948 with no clear outside challenge.

The second thing, closely related, is that the central government in the North has almost unlimited power. The Korean Workers' Party is the only political organization with any power in the Democratic People's Republic. This strong central control reaches into every corner of daily life. It controls what foods will be available, what is to be taught in the schools, and what is going to be seen on television or heard on the radio, for televisions and radios are limited to receiving only the approved frequencies. This, from a Western point of view, seems an intolerably high price in restrictions on personal freedoms for the visible results.

The Korean Workers' Party stresses its allegiance to Marxism-Leninism and uses this ideology as a means of bringing in and holding together the people. Slogans such as "steel-like unity" are used to suggest a unity of purpose that finds its best expression in the "thoughts of our great leader, Kim Il Sung" and, as his son is being prepared to succeed him, the thoughts and deeds of the "dear leader," Kim Jong Il.

The individual who does not go along with the approved way of doing things faces arrest, punishment, even death at the worst. At the least, he or she faces long sessions of self-criticism, confessing errors and mistakes publicly to friends and associates, becoming a target of disap-

P'yŏngyang street; shoppers passing in front of a clothing store.   Se Hoon Park/The Korea Times U.S.A.

Passengers waiting for a train at Sŏnch'ŏnyŏk Railway Station. Se Hoon Park/The Korea Times U.S.A.

proval. For those to whom the security of the group is more important than the freedom of the individual, there are real economic, social, and psychological rewards to be gained by adherence to a single doctrine and serving a single master. The individual can come to feel an important part of the process of helping the nation reach its goals.

Chuch'e

Kim Il Sung is held up as a hero to the people of North Korea. They are seldom out of sight of his portrait or out of earshot of his wisdom, which most often is directed toward the national ideal of self-sufficiency—a Korean Korea economically, intellectually, and spiritually—free of outside interference.

The Tower of the Juche Idea stands on the bank of the Taedong River in Pyongyang. The Korean people are moving ahead confidently towards the complete victory of the revolutionary cause of Juche. They erected it to immortalize the ideo-theoretical and revolutionary exploits of the great leader President Kim Il Sung, father of the immortal Juche idea.

Height of the tower:

	170 metres
Tower body:	150 metres
Torch:	20 metres

MONUMENTAL STRUCTURE

The Tower of the Juche Idea

Sculptured groups

There are monuments everywhere to Kim Il Sung, his ideas, or his past actions. Here the Tower of the Juche *(Chuch'e)* Idea *in P'yŏngyang from the January 1989 issue of* Korea Today.

In 1955 Kim Il Sung elaborated his principle of *chuch'e*, which he developed further in an address to the Fourth Congress of the Korean Workers' Party in 1961:

By *chuch'e* we mean that in carrying out our revolution and construction we should creatively apply the general truth of Marxism-Leninism to the specific realities of our own country, and precisely and fully take into account our own historical and actual situation, our own capacity, and the traditions, the requirements, and the level of consciousness of our own people.

The idea that Marxist ideology should be in this sense subordinate to Korea's national identity is apparent in all activities, from the teaching of children in schools to performances in the national theater.

But on a more practical level than this, the *chuch'e* ideal has allowed the development of a system of education and control that is loosely supported by traditional family and clan practices. More than a quarter of the total population is enrolled in schools of some sort. From kindergarten up, children learn the principles of a Marxist state molded upon the principle of *chuch'e*, a specifically *Korean* Communist state growing out of the ideas of Kim Il Sung.

In a poem, "Party," the poet Pak Chong-sik suggests some of the positives of the Party. This is hardly poetry to a Western taste, but it does read as heartfelt, if naïve, praise poetry.

This poem
I write and rewrite,
And write again a hundred times,
Is for you, Party,
You, quickening and beating in my heart.

Though I have given you nothing
You have favored me
With great kindness.

As a child
I cried with poverty and hunger;
As a youth
I trembled under persecution and humiliation.

Party!
You beat back all those sad things,
Cut the chains of oppression from my wrists,
Gave me true liberty.
And, with my brush held high,
You made me sing the world
At the limits of heart and voice.

The flowing streams,
Towering peaks,
Boundless plains,
Golden factories,
Thanks to you
Not one that is not mine.

For the people of North Korea, there is little or none of the contact with the world that intrudes on the West daily. Media and personal movement are both strictly controlled. Pak Chong-sik makes no comparison in his poem except with the past, as he knows it through living and what he has been taught in school. Without a basis for comparison, criticism does not exist except in the most negative way. Only through comparison with some other country could the situation of the North come into clearer focus. That opportunity has been limited to a select few.

When P'yŏngyang held the Thirteenth Annual Youth Games in 1988, the North Korean people saw it as a major international event being hosted by their government. North Korean magazines ran car-

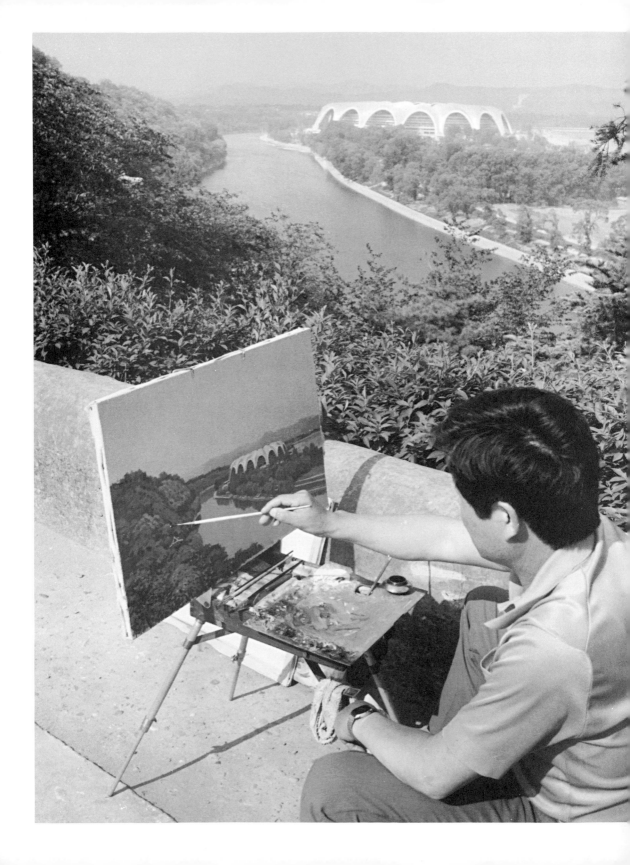

toons contrasting the "peace games" in P'yŏngyang with the "war games"—the summer Olympics—in Seoul. But beyond that kind of dismissive commentary they had no sense of what the rest of the world was seeing. The Youth Games, as far as they were concerned, were the major event. To most of the rest of the world they were only a small underreported event in the Third World, overshadowed by the glamor of the successful summer Olympics in Seoul. The success of the Seoul Olympics may have gotten through as a kind of disturbing whisper to North Koreans, but the Youth Games were a deafening success.

The North Korean authorities got what they wanted to help keep their control of their people: The P'yŏngyang Youth Games masked the Seoul Olympics from view. But where the Olympic Games in Seoul opened a whole new world of international promise to the government and people of the Republic of Korea, the Games in P'yŏngyang once again served only to emphasize the stubborn isolation of the People's Republic and raise again the question of how long that isolation can be maintained in today's rapidly changing world.

An artist painting a picture of the main stadium for the Thirteenth World Festival of Youth and Students from the Moranbong, a famous viewpoint on a bluff overlooking the Taedong River. Se Hoon Park/The Korea Times U.S.A.

Village and City, North and South

You who are drunk on worldly ambition,
consider the future.
A naked child
thinks only of the sunlight,
but when the sun crosses west mountain
what then can the child do?
Kim Su-jang; translation by Kevin O'Rourke

Continuity Within Change

Korea today remains a ferment; the yeast of modernization is still working. An ancient civilization that was never as static as some have thought has been changing with unprecedented speed. Gregory Henderson, a long-time observer of the Korean scene, observed that the Korean has ". . . seen within the span of a contemporary human lifetime historical changes more frequent and complete than the total of those which history visited upon the peninsula from the seventh to the nineteenth century."

North and South, the changes seem profound, at least on the surface. Yet visitors to the North remark on a sense of old formalities still observed, a feeling in day-to-day, person-to-person contacts that things are somehow more as they were before revolution and social restructuring than in the South. In the South, visitors note the loss of much of that old formality, a growing brusqueness and indifference coupled with untoward familiarities in everyday life. Yet the same observer of the South will note with appreciation and excitement the widespread interest in the folk arts, traditional dance, music, and painting—all of which are officially disparaged, except for study, in the North as being representative of a feudal and repressive society.

This is typical of the mixed feelings that accompany great change—a longing for a past that was familiar and comfortable in the face of a troubling present. In the South the same energy that nurtures major

Break time along the road in the Mohyang Mountain area near P'yŏngyang. Tractor and trailer are manufactured in North Korea.   Se Hoon Park/The Korea Times U.S.A.

business and fuels industry seems also to propel students and people to constant revolt: to a violence in search of peace and freedom that has, in the long run, served to keep the governments honest. In the North the same energies seem to be spent in the glorification of the Great Leader and his son, the Beloved Leader, and a tightening of central controls.

Both South and North Koreans not only know they are Koreans, they take pride in being Korean. The separation is political and ideological, a product in part of the cold war, in part of the lack of charismatic leadership for all Korea at that crucial point on August 15, 1945, when Japan surrendered.

The theme of self-reliance, of *chuch'e*, as articulated in the North, is

Schoolboys in their school uniforms transplanting rice in the paddies. Another work team is making its way across the dikes between the paddies in the rear. North Korea. Se Hoon Park/The Korea Times U.S.A.

not unlike the demands for self-determination and self-sufficiency made by political and moral leaders in the South. The proposed means, of course, differ. This idea of self-sufficiency is, in practical terms, an impossible ideal, even for a unified peninsula. Neither North nor South has the potential to stand alone. And while they have taken different paths, they have wound up in much the same place: industrialized, urbanized economies and societies that, better sooner than later, need to find a niche in the world economy.

South Korea moved early to an accommodation with the industrialized nations of the capitalist West; North Korea, tied to the socialist world economy, has moved more slowly. Today as the communist world is being reshaped by events in Eastern Europe and the Soviet Union, it will be a test of North Korea's flexibility as to how those changes are accommodated.

City and Country

In the wake of war and industrialization, many of the villages that were once the heart of an agricultural nation are only shells of what they were even twenty years ago. In the South, young men and women have left for the cities and for jobs in the growing manufacturing industries, where the pay is usually better than in the villages, where they are now no longer needed on the newly mechanized farms. In the North, state and party have assigned them to where they are most needed.

Yet the poet Yi Hyŏn-bo's lament from five centuries ago still rings true: "Back to the village, all say it, but no one goes back. . . ." The farmer rated very high in the traditional Confucian scheme of things, and though everyone knows there is no way to go back to the farm in this modern industrialized world, there is a strong nostalgic pull to the village. There is a Korean word, *kohyang*, that is often translated

In the corner of the yard in any traditional Korean house near the kitchen will be found a collection of earthenware crocks of various sizes. These are used for making sauces, such as soy sauce, and storage of preserved foods such as kimchi. *Pressure-activated pumps and spigots have replaced buckets on the ends of ropes as a means to draw water from the well. North Chŏlla Province.* Hyungwon Kang

"hometown" but means much more than that. It means the place where a person's ancestors' tombs are located; the place the family has its roots; and for most Koreans until well into the twentieth century, that meant somewhere in the countryside.

In South Korea, at least, at *Ch'usŏk*, or the Autumn Moon Festival, the cities drain into the countryside in a rush that clogs all routes of transportation from the trains to family cars. The villages, particularly the village cemeteries, become centers of intense activities as scattered families gather to pay their respects to the ancestors at the family tombs. For the moment it can seem as if the city has returned to the village.

Changing Families

Family in the West usually means only mother, father, and children. This has not been true of the Korean family in the past, though things are changing today. Many households would have had three generations represented, sometimes even four. When the eldest son of a family married, he brought his wife home to live with him. As long as his parents were alive, they all lived together. His children remained, in turn, and should his eldest son marry before the grandparents died, that son and his wife would move in as well.

While apartment dwellers in modern cities clearly cannot accommodate this kind of a household, there remains a kind of ideal of the

Maintaining the ancestral tombs. Members of the photographer's mother's family work on one of the tombs at the family burial site, where twelve generations of the main line of the family are interred. Hyungwon Kang

traditional family that is reinforced by the same Confucian pattern of relationships, which even today follows old ideals.

In practice, this can lead to the father's being isolated from his children and even from his wife. He is the head of the family, the disciplinarian, and the one to whom all loyalty is due. Making all major decisions, he carries on the family business with outside society, often without much consultation with wife or children. A fully traditional father would not think of consulting them, although he might turn to his father or some older man for advice.

Today in South Korea, women have the right to vote and, particularly in the cities, are going into the professions. Under the traditional pattern they had no equality with men. Women were, and are, to be loyal to their husbands first of all, but loyalty is not enough. They are expected to bear children, and in traditional Korean society a woman was hardly thought to have borne a child until she had borne a son. The son is necessary to carry on the family, to maintain that ritual continuity of past and future that is so important in the Confucian system.

But despite the seemingly unequal position of the woman, she does have considerable power within the home, if not outside. It is she to whom the children turn with their troubles, she who determines the food and clothing and the operation of the household. And often in the process she will keep tight hold on the family purse strings.

Given this traditional emphasis on children and particularly the Confucian sense that a son was necessary, it is somewhat surprising to see that the Republic of Korea has had one of the most effective programs of family planning and population control in the world. The opposite has been true in the North, where a shortage of labor has led to a drive to encourage large families, and where, in a socialist state, women have full equality with men, at least insofar as they are able to work in each and every job alongside men. But the old patterns are still maintained. Dr. Chung found himself inscribed as family head, patriarch, when he visited his mother's grave in North Korea and was greeted and treated as the head of a family he had not seen or heard from for thirty-three years.

Two Cities: Seoul

City life North or South does not reflect the regular cycle of the seasons that governs a farmer's life. Summer or winter, the day goes on much the same. The pattern is determined by occupation, vocation, avocation: the many pressures of day-to-day living. Yet today it is here in the city next to the government offices, factories, universities, and research centers that the greater proportion of the Korean people live, work, and die. Here today's world impinges most heavily upon tradition; here

Seoul looking south over City Hall. To the left is Namsan, the South Mountain, and directly down the street is Namdaemun, the Great South Gate, which once closed a walled city off from the outside, now dwarfed by the modern city around it. Hyungwon Kang

individuals are trying to find their own ways, to pick and choose as they will from old traditions for the making of a new Korea.

In the South, where there is no strong revolutionary center pulling things together, society at times seems to spin off into the chaos of student protests, the crime and disruption that are a part of city life everywhere, and the terrible search for what is right when the very ideas of right and wrong seem to be changing and there is no concrete authority. Surprisingly, more seems to come right than go wrong. Widespread student and middle-class citizen protests in 1988 led to a constitutional change that allowed for the direct election of the president in the following elections, a major step toward greater democratic freedom.

In the North it is different. There is the indisputable ideological center around the Great Leader, Kim Il Sung, who directs everything down to the most intimate acts of personal life. There has been so far no open evidence of popular resistance; there are no students waving the flag of reunification or protesting police brutality or clashing with police on the streets of P'yŏngyang; nor is there any middle class, in this purportedly classless society, to join in their protest.

Korea's two great cities have always been Seoul and P'yŏngyang, and so they remain, unchallenged despite the appearance of many other large metropolitan centers, both North and South, with their growing populations and increasing industrialization. Both cities were severely damaged by the Korean War. Both have rebuilt, but on radically different patterns.

Seoul, which has been the capital of Korea since 1392, and has remained the capital of the Republic of Korea, is a sprawling megalopolis with a skyline that changes more rapidly even than those of modern American cities. With a population approaching eleven million, it is one of the largest cities in the world, and one of the most cosmopolitan. It is a city where there is more new than old, yet where the old creeps

Myŏngdong, the center of Seoul, with a typical line of street vendors. Hyungwon Kang

through and gives it that touch of individuality and depth of character that makes the city fascinating.

There are old palaces, ancient royal tombs, fortresses, the gates of the old city wall, the fortifications of ancient Paekche that were incorporated into Olympic Park, and much else to remind the passerby of ancient Korea.

There is also the hurry and hustle of a modern metropolis plagued with the fumes and fears of environmental pollution that come with a technology that seemingly cannot plan, except for its own destruction. People go in all directions in the morning: businessmen off to their offices; clerks, secretaries, shop girls all rushing to make their bus or subway connections; schoolboys and girls off to class.

Carrying all her personal belongings in the apronlike bag around her waist and her small stock of goods in the aluminum basin on her head, this homeless vendor sets out to find a good spot on downtown Seoul streets.   Hyungwon Kang

The Great South Gate is veiled with confetti during an annual Military Day parade in downtown Seoul. Seoul was a walled city until the end of the nineteenth century, with gates that closed at night. This gate marked the southern edge of the city.   Hyungwon Kang

At the turn of the century, Seoul was a city of around a quarter million, and even then it was growing out of its environs. The population had spilled over the wall that Yi Sŏng-gye had built around his capital city five centuries before. Today most of that wall has disappeared, except for sections running across the mountains to the north and south of the center of the city. The two great gates that still remain—Namdaemun, the Great South Gate, and Tongdaemun, the Great East Gate—today stand in the center of the city.

Yet when Korea was liberated from Japan in 1945, this was a city of perhaps a million and a half, one tenth its present size. The Korean War reduced that population to less than half a million and much of the city to rubble. Out of these ruins the vital core of the city began to grow. In the early 1960's there were no buildings in Seoul more than ten stories high, almost none with central heating or air conditioning. Electricity and water were limited, and in most areas available only for brief periods during the day. Indoor plumbing was a luxury, as were private cars and telephones.

In the late 1960's and throughout the 1970's the city began to grow at an unbelievable rate. Buildings of twenty stories and more began to spring up along newly widened streets. A subway system was installed; expressways and paved roads linked Seoul as the center to the rest of South Korea. By the early 1980's the population had grown to 8.5 million.

The city continues to grow, supported by a foreign-trade economy and the rapidly expanding manufacturing of high-technology products (electronics, computers, televisions, VCRs) as well as steel and iron. It is also

The end of a dynasty: The funeral procession of Princess Yi Pangja, the wife of Crown Prince Yi Un, last of the Yi Dynasty aspirants to the throne, leaves the Naksŏnjae. She was Japanese, once considered a possible wife to Emperor Hirohito. Since their son, who has become an American citizen, was never crowned prince, her death marked the end of the direct line of Yi Dynasty rulers. Hyungwon Kang

The annual celebration of Confucius's birthday at the Sŏnggyun'gwan University in Seoul. Note the participation of women in the ceremony, something that would have been unheard of in traditional times.   Hyungwon Kang

the world's largest manufacturer of party hats and other novelty headgear.

It is a city of palaces and universities as well as business towers, hotels, and Olympic arenas. Yet here too tradition strives against the changes that are being made. The Sŏnggyun'gwan University stands beside the palace grounds where kings lived and ruled, where prince and princess played in the gardens, and the royal family enjoyed the changes of flowers through the year and the colors of autumn. In Yi times the Sŏnggyun'gwan was the highest center for study in the nation. It was there that the principal shrine to Confucius was maintained. To the Sŏnggyun'gwan also came the best of the young scholars from the local schools to complete their studies under the tutelage of the greatest minds of their times.

Today the Sŏnggyun'gwan is a modern university, offering courses similar to those taught in any college of arts and sciences in the United States. True, it has a college of Oriental philosophy where there is a strong emphasis on the study of Confucianism; but the only real reminder of its illustrious past is the national shrine to Confucius on the university grounds, where the elaborate ceremony honoring him is held each autumn.

Two Cities: P'yŏngyang

P'yŏngyang is the cultural and political center of the Democratic People's Republic of Korea, just as Seoul is of the South. Here are the major offices of government, the headquarters of the armed forces, the center of the movie industry, and the homes of artists, musicians, and dancers. The landscape is dominated by images of the "Great Leader," Kim Il Sung, with reminders that it is his beneficence that has made all this possible.

In contrast to those of Seoul, the streets of P'yŏngyang are relatively empty of cars. It is only when people are on their way to work that the streets bustle with pedestrians and bicycles. There are buses, trucks, and bicycles, but many fewer automobiles than in Seoul—only some Russian-built limousines reserved for special government use and a few Mercedes for driving foreign visitors around. Workers, often shirtless, jog or walk in formation along the broad streets on their way to work, singing or chanting. Children march briskly in loose formation on their way to school, singing patriotic songs. The bulk of the morning rush is carried by the very modern Metro, the subway system. Privately owned automobiles, commonplace in Seoul, are unknown here. The buildings that in South Korea or in the West would house businesses here are apartments for the workers.

P'yŏngyang today is a city of broad avenues and well-tended streets. The greater part of the city proper has been rebuilt since the Korean War. There has been no tenfold growth of population as there was in Seoul. From around 600,000 people at the end of the Korean War, P'yŏngyang has grown to about a million and a quarter today. And even that growth has been more controlled and directed than that in Seoul.

There are department stores and special shops where the basic needs of day-to-day living are supplied as well as a limited range of consumer

Overview of P'yŏngyang, the capital of the Democratic People's Republic of Korea. Center rear is the 150,000-seat main stadium for the Thirteenth World Festival of Youth and Students. Se Hoon Park/The Korea Times U.S.A.

goods. The basic needs of the people are being met, and there are even some nonessential consumer goods in the shops of P'yŏngyang, but none of the variety, nor any of the luxury items that can be found in Seoul. Most shops accommodate late-shift workers by staying open until ten in the evening.

There is none of the advertising that clutters the thoroughfares of cities in the South and so much more of the world, for this is not a competitive economy; the government determines what is to be produced, in what quantity, and how and where it is to be sold.

Near the National Theater is a park where children play as they wait to enter to see a performance, or to rehearse one of their own. There is much emphasis on pageantry and group activity. People are brought together to see performances and participate in dramas and operas depicting the successes of the revolution and the victory of communist right over imperialist wrong.

P'yŏngyang is an older city than Seoul. Its past greatness dates from before the five hundred years of the Yi Dynasty. While the North Korean capital does preserve, and to some extent revere, the remains of its "feudal" past, its eyes are more on the present and future. It is, after all, the home of a revolution that was to cut off the evils of the past and make a new start, guided by the *chuch'e* thought of the "Great Leader."

Two Cities

The contrasts between the two capitals are often extreme. Seoul gives the impression of an unpruned plant sprawling every which way, including up; P'yŏngyang, a sense of ordered and planned development. While the hurrying crowds in the streets of Seoul suggest a kind of purposeful confusion, those of P'yŏngyang reflect an ordered purposefulness that might more properly be described as regimented. The cities themselves reflect two very different styles of life, rooted in the same cultural past, that have developed out of the political and philosophical differences between the governments of the Republic of Korea and the Democratic People's Republic of Korea.

In Closing

To the north of Paektu Mountain on the Manchurian Highlands live some 2.5 million Koreans in the Autonomous Korean Region of the People's Republic of China. There are several hundred thousand Koreans still in Soviet Siberia, and several hundred thousand more in the Soviet Middle East, where they were relocated by the Stalinist government in the Soviet Union. The Korean American population is fast approaching a million. Some of the finest Korean restaurants in the world are in Los Angeles; Seoul-style noodles are to be had on the road across Manchuria to Paektu Mountain. There are Korean traders and entrepreneurs on all the continents. What was not so long ago an obscure peninsula in northeast Asia has, in its southern portion, become a major manufacturing and trading country.

Both North and South Korea required massive quantities of foreign aid to recover from forty years of colonial domination and the war that came so shortly after liberation. But South or North, that is only a part of the story. The major burden of recovery fell upon the shoulders of the Korean people themselves; and while suffering under repressive governments and from the worst violations of human rights and dignity, they still managed to create modern nations. It has been said that the Economic Miracle on the Han, as South Korea's recovery has been called, was built on the labor of South Korea's women as they were brought onto the assembly lines and into the sweatshop clothing factories at incredibly low wages for unbelievably long hours. There was a

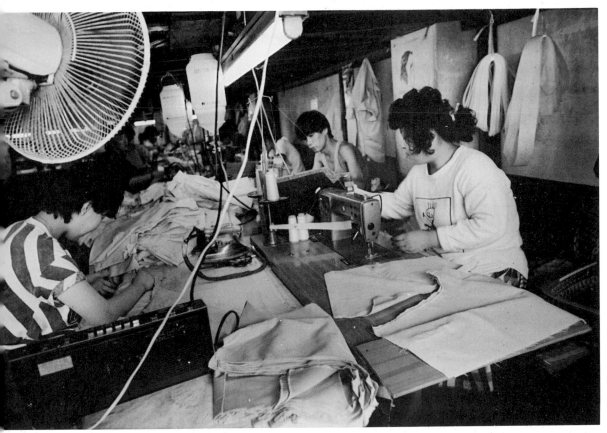

South Korea has become a world center for the manufacture of clothing. Much of that industry is based upon small sweatshop operations such as this one in the Chŏnggyejŏn District of Seoul, where the employees work extemely long hours under miserable conditions for minimal wages.   Hyungwon Kang

major investment in education and training of a skilled and semiskilled labor force, many of them also women, that made South Korea ready very early on to join in the international electronics revolution. To become a trading country, South Korea, with its limited natural resources, needed something to trade. For South Korea, that became cheap labor, employed both in Korean factories and abroad, in the labor force that accompanied Korean construction companies into the oil-rich Middle East. To trade, of course, requires trading partners, and the South has been opening more and more doors, even to the formerly socialist countries of Eastern Europe.

Koreans Abroad

But there has been a price to pay for all this, and a part of it is reflected in the story of that international community as it has grown up outside the Korean peninsula for the past hundred years or so. The first Koreans in Siberia and Manchuria in modern times fled their homeland ahead of famine and disruption during the last decades of the Yi Dynasty. They were followed across the next forty years by their countrymen fleeing the Japanese aggressor.

A few made their way to the United States, most as laborers on the Hawaiian sugar plantations from 1904 to 1905, a few hundred more later as students or picture brides—young women who married men already overseas on the promise of a picture until they met at the dock in Honolulu or the West Coast of the United States. The great cause of the Korean in exile was the freedom of the homeland. But with freedom came division, war, and the repressive governments of both North and South.

The human price of economic development is not often calculated. The accountants' balance sheets do not have entries for deaths, exiles, or lost freedoms. But the constant stream of Koreans into the United States since the 1960's has been a new exile for many of the same reasons.

Unlike those first Korean immigrants to this country, these new immigrants do not meet to plan the liberation of the homeland. They become American citizens and work as well and as fully as they can to grasp the opportunity they see in this land and to fulfill their responsi-

Prior to 1987 South Korean labor unions had little independence and were subject to strict government control. A series of strikes such as this one at a Hyundai Heavy Industries plant in Ulsan helped the unions gain more independence and bargaining power.
Hyungwon Kang

bilities to a new citizenship. They have found room to breathe away from the often stifling restrictions of their South Korean homeland. North Korea does not allow its citizens to emigrate.

But be it in Uzbekistan, Siberia, or Los Angeles, Koreans remain Korean. They bring with them their food, their language, their customs, and on ceremonial occasions their costumes. They bring as well an awareness of a homeland divided between South and North, of families still separated, of ties with the ancestral lands and graves still severed. The tragedy of divisions is borne by every Korean, no matter where. Korea runs from Paektu Mountain to Mount Halla on Cheju Island. The division between the Republic of Korea and the Democratic People's Republic of Korea is less than half a century old, less than a moment in the history of a land that counts its beginnings from 2,000 years ago.

The Korean people have always endured, often despite their leaders; they will continue to endure, looking forward to that day when their land will be whole again and their individual lives will also be that much fuller.

Bibliography

Bibliographies

For a well-annotated selective bibliography of works in English, see pp. 395–413 of Ki-baik Lee's *A New History of Korea* below, under *Histories*. For more detailed bibliographies:

Kim, Han-Kyo. *Studies on Korea: A Scholar's Guide.* Honolulu: University Press of Hawaii, 1980.

Marcus, Richard, ed. *Korean Studies Guide.* Berkeley: University of California Press, 1954.

Handbooks

For current news and information about Korea, North and South, such sources as the *Britannica Book of the Year*, *The World Almanac*, and many other similar year-books or periodical surveys are helpful. There are also such books as *A Handbook of Korea* issued irregularly by the Korean Overseas Information Service. This is a broad-ranging collection of encyclopedialike essays on topics from Korean history to tourism today. The emphasis, of course, is on the Republic of Korea. Other survey-type books are the North and South Korea volumes in the Area Handbook Series prepared for the Department of the Army.

Bunge, Frederica M., ed. *North Korea: A Country Study.* Washington: U.S. Government Printing Office, 1982.

————. *South Korea: A Country Study.* Washington: U.S. Government Printing Office, 1982.

Korean Overseas Information Service. *A Handbook of Korea.* Seoul: Seoul International Publishing House, 1987.

Journals

There are several periodicals of interest. *Korea Journal*, published by the Korean National Commission of UNESCO, carries a variety of articles, from the highly specialized scholarly study to reviews of contemporary theater and comments on daily life in South Korea. *Korea Journal* consistently publishes translations from Korean literature; it is one of the few places where such translations can be found. *Korean Culture* is a quarterly magazine published by the Korean Cultural Service in Los Angeles. Its focus has been more on Korean art, though it does publish the occasional translation and other kinds of articles as well. *The Korea Herald* newspaper publishes and distributes in the United States both an English- and a Korean-language version of *Korea Photo*, with short, photojournalistic stories on South Korean life and places. Harder to find are *Democratic People's Republic of Korea*, a photojoural edited and published in P'yŏngyang, and *Korea Today*, also published in P'yŏngyang, which includes some translations and more extended stories about life in North Korea. With the exception of the UNESCO *Korea Journal*, these are all official or quasi-official publications of the governments involved. Keeping everything in perspective can be a nice exercise in critical reading. There is also the *Korea Times U.S.A. Magazine*, published weekly in Los Angeles, which deals mostly with Korean American topics.

Democratic People's Republic of Korea, edited and published by *Korea Pictorial*. P'yŏngyang: Foreign Languages Publishing House.

Korea Journal. Korean National Commission for UNESCO, P.O. Box Central 64, Seoul, Republic of Korea.

Korea Photo. The Korea Herald Subscription Service, P.O. Box 312, Hartsdale, NY 10530.

The Korea Times U.S.A. Magazine. The Korea Times, 141 North Vermont Ave., Los Angeles, CA 90004.

Korea Today. P'yŏngyang: The Foreign Language Magazines. Foreign Languages Publishing House.

Korean Culture. The Korean Cultural Service, 5505 Wilshire Blvd., Los Angeles, CA 90036.

Histories

The most readable of the general histories is probably:

Han, Woo-Kuen. *The History of Korea.* Translated by Kyong-shik Lee, edited by Grafton K. Mintz. Honolulu: University Press of Hawaii, 1971.

While this next book is somewhat denser but still quite readable:

Lee, Ki-baik. *A New History of Korea.* Translated by Edward W. Wagner with Edward J. Shultz. Cambridge, MA: Harvard University Press, 1984.

For a more detailed cultural history, which can be pretty hard going in spots:

Joe, Wanne J. *Traditional Korea: A Cultural History.* Seoul: Chungang University Press, 1972.

More fun, though much less systematic, is:

Rutt, Richard. *James Scarth Gale's History of the Korean People.* Seoul: Royal Asiatic Society, Korea Branch, 1975.

For a sense of how the Korean monk and historian of the thirteenth century looked at the world, see the wonderful collection of tales and legends in:

Iryŏn. *Samguk Yusa: Legends and History of the Three Kingdoms of Ancient Korea.* Translated by Tae-Hung Ha and Grafton K. Mintz. Seoul: Yonsei University Press, 1972.

Some of the more interesting books—which in some cases have to be read with care, since they were written by participants in the events described—for the period from the opening of Korea's ports down to liberation from Japanese rule are:

Chung, Henry. *The Case of Korea.* New York: Revell, 1921.
—a step-by-step documentation of the Japanese movement into Korea and the following uprising in 1919.

Dealing with the earlier years, from the 1880's down to the turn of the century, is a study of the role of the American medical missionary and diplomat Horace Allen:

Harrington, Fred Harvey. *God, Mammon, and the Japanese: Dr. Horace N. Allen and Korean-American Relations, 1884–1905.* Madison: University of Wisconsin Press, 1944.

The same period is described by one of Dr. Allen's contemporaries, an American missionary and educator who participated in or witnessed many of the events:

Hulbert, Homer B. *The Passing of Korea.* New York: Doubleday, 1906. Reprinted by Yonsei University Press in Seoul, 1969.

Korea's attempt to keep the Japanese out from 1876 down through the March First Movement in 1919 was given sympathetic treatment by a Canadian journalist in two books:

McKenzie, Frederick A. *Korea's Fight for Freedom.* New York: Revell, 1920. Reprinted by Yonsei University Press in Seoul, 1969.

————. *The Tragedy of Korea.* London: Hodder & Stoughton, 1908. Reprinted by Yonsei University Press in 1969.

There is one convenient short historical survey of modern Korea, concentrating mostly on the years since 1880 and into the 1980's:

Rees, David. *A Short History of Modern Korea.* Port Erin, Isle of Man: Ham Publishing Company Limited, 1988.

Otherwise, most of the accounts of the post-1945 years tend to be quite specialized. Since the Republic of Korea has been tied so closely to the United States, it is of interest to look at a book that deals in some detail with problems that have been major irritants in that relationship—the Reverend Sun Myong Moon and the "Moonies," and what was known at the time as "Koreagate":

Boettcher, Robert, and Gordon L. Freedman. *Gifts of Deceit: Sun Myong Moon, Tongsun Park and the Korean Scandal.* New York: Holt, 1980.

No American knew the Korean scene of the late 1940's better than Gregory Henderson, and that interest continued through his service as a U.S. Foreign Service officer in Korea and until his recent death. Parts of his book are turgid with theory, but when he shifts to narrative accounts of events as he experienced them, the writing is compelling:

Henderson, Gregory. *Korea: The Politics of the Vortex.* Cambridge, MA: Harvard University Press, 1968.

A postscript to the Yi Dynasty and a touching account of the lives of royal families, mostly Korean but also Japanese, is the life story of the Japanese princess who was chosen to marry the last Yi crown prince:

Yi Pangja. *The World Is One: Princess Yi Pangja's Autobiography.* Translated by Sokkyu Kim. Seoul: Taewon Publishing Company, 1973.

There is little written about North Korea that is not highly speculative or theoretical. The earliest firsthand accounts by recent visitors, Korean Americans, came in the early 1980's. The first was by a well-known Korean American writer:

Hyun, Peter. *Darkness at Dawn: A North Korean Diary.* Seoul: Hanjin Publishing Company, 1981.
—in which he recorded his impressions of not only North Korea but also the Korean communities of Northern China.

Following close after came a volume of essays by seven Korean American (all Korean-born) university professors who visited North Korea in 1981:

Kim, C. I. Eugene, and B. C. Koh, eds. *Journey to North Korea: Personal Perceptions.* Berkeley: Institute of East Asian Studies, 1983.

A third book is an autobiographical account of growing up in the Korean community in Harbin, Manchuria, during the Japanese occupation and in North Korea in the years after liberation. The author also describes his immigration to the U.S. and his highly emotional return home for a reunion with his surviving sisters.

Chung, Donald K., M.D. *The Three Day Promise: A Korean Soldier's Memoir.* Tallahassee, FL: Father and Son Publishing, 1989.

For a comprehensive, and at times exhausting, overview of the Korean War:

Rees, David. *Korea: The Limited War.* New York: St. Martin's, 1964.

An eyewitness account of the beginning of the Korean War by a U.S. embassy officer is:

Noble, Harold Joyce. *Embassy at War.* Edited with an Introduction by Frank P. Baldwin, Jr. Seattle: University of Washington Press, 1975.

Personal experiences of several important Koreans while Seoul was occupied by the North Koreans are incorporated into a scholarly framework in:

Riley, John W., and Wilbur Schramm. *The Reds Take a City: The Communist Occupation of Seoul, with Eyewitness Accounts.* New Brunswick, NJ: Rutgers University Press, 1951.

Geography

The best easily available geography of Korea is:

McCune, Shannon. *Korea's Heritage: A Regional & Social Geography.* Tokyo and Rutland, VT: Tuttle, 1956.

Art and Literature

For a comprehensive overview of Korean art:

Kim, Chewon, and Lena Kim Lee. *Arts of Korea.* Tokyo: Kodansha International, 1974.

A good introduction to Korean folktales is:

Carpenter, Frances. *Tales of a Korean Grandmother.* Tokyo and Rutland, VT: Tuttle, 1973.

or:

Zong, In-sob. *Folk Tales from Korea.* Elizabeth, NJ: Hollym International, 1970.

An autobiographical tale of growing up in the rapidly changing world of early twentieth-century Korea is:

Kang, Younghill. *The Grass Roof.* New York: Scribner, 1931, with a reprint, Chicago: Follett, 1966.

Another autobiographical novel from a somewhat later time is:

Kim, Richard. *Lost Names: Scenes from a Korean Boyhood.* New York: Praeger, 1970.

Probably the best introduction to modern Korean poetry is that of the poet

Ko Won, compiler and translator. *Contemporary Korean Poetry.* Iowa City: University of Iowa Press, 1970.

For a good introduction to the modern short story:

O'Rourke, Kevin, translator. *A Washed-Out Dream.* Larchmont, NY: Larchwood Publications, 1973.

For the traditional *sijo*:

Rutt, Richard. *The Bamboo Grove: An Introduction to Sijo.* Berkeley: University of California Press, 1971.

For traditional fiction:

Rutt, Richard, and Chong-un Kim, translators. *Virtuous Women: Three Masterpieces of Korean Fiction.* Seoul: Korean National Commission for UNESCO, 1974.

Daily Life

There are a number of anthropological and sociological studies of Korean life, most of them quite technical. Many do have narrative sections that make for very interesting reading. These kinds of books can be located through the bibliographies listed above or in library card catalogs. There are other books, more relaxed, sometimes casual notes of day-to-day observations, at other times more seriously intended, that do make good introductory reading. Among them, a book by a medical missionary and long-time resident of Korea:

Crane, Paul. *Korean Patterns.* Seoul: Royal Asiatic Society, Korea Branch, 1978.

Or the life histories included in the more technical work of an anthropologist:

Harvey, Youngsook Kim. *Six Korean Women: The Socialization of Shamans.* St. Paul, MN: West Publishing Company, 1979.

Then there are the various essays in:

Mattielli, Sandra, ed. *Virtues in Conflict: Tradition and the Korean Woman Today.* Seoul: Samhwa, 1977.

And the delightful reminiscences of Bishop Rutt:

Rutt, Richard. *Korean Works and Days: Notes from the Diary of a Country Priest.* Seoul: Royal Asiatic Society, Korea Branch, 1964, reprinted 1978.

Index

Numbers in *italics* refer to illustrations.